Julia felt the bed bounce as she fell back, and Samantha was on top of her. Samantha's mouth consumed her. Samantha broke contact for a moment to drag Julia's clothes off, then her mouth was at Julia's breasts — her tongue tracing along the edge of her bra, her teeth gently teasing Julia's swollen nipples through the lace. Julia clasped Samantha's shoulders tightly as her lust increased.

Samantha's fingers were trailing up the inside of her thigh, leaving a fiery wake, and then she stroked her — just once between her thighs. Julia gasped. Suddenly, Samantha's fingers thrust inside her. Julia groaned, closed her eyes, felt her hips rise. Samantha's fingers plunged more deeply. Her mind went blank as a powerful heat pumped through her body. She couldn't stop gasping. She reached down to feel Samantha's hand, her wet fingers thrusting into her, then they withdrew a little and stilled, applying pressure inside her, her thumb outside, stroking her.

Julia felt herself rising to a peak of electrifying tension that was surpassed again and again. It was as if she were flying at an incredible speed through a dark night to a place she'd never been.

Julia's Song

BY
ANN O'LEARY

THE NAIAD PRESS, INC.
1998

Printed in the United States of America on acid-free paper
First Edition

Editor: Christine Cassidy
Cover designer: Bonnie Liss (Phoenix Graphics)
Typesetter: Sandi Stancil

Library of Congress Cataloging-in-Publication Data

O'Leary, Ann, 1955 –
   Julia's song / by Ann O'Leary.
      p.   cm.
   ISBN 1-56280-197-X (pbk.)
   I. Title.
PR9619.3.0386J8 1998
823—dc21

97-52749
CIP

For Helen

ABOUT THE AUTHOR

Ann O'Leary was born in Melbourne, Australia, where she lives with her partner. Ann's career began in film production, diverged into TV advertising, then for several years, she was a producer working with her partner in their own audio production company. Ann is now a full-time writer. Her previous book, *Letting Go,* was also published by Naiad Press.

CHAPTER ONE

Julia Moran made her way to her seat in the press gallery. The Melbourne Concert Hall was packed to full capacity and the applause was deafening. The opening act, an all-women blues band, had just finished their performance and were leaving the stage. They seemed to have primed the audience well for the main event. Julia saw the photographer, who was working with her tonight, at the other end of the gallery which ran along one side of the stage, and gave him a wave. As she settled into her seat, the applause subsided, replaced by the clamor of thousands of excited voices.

The house lights came on and Julia looked around. The concert-goers were wriggling in their seats, calling out to their friends and laughing and talking loudly. The atmosphere was electric with anticipation. Julia wasn't surprised to see that the audience was almost entirely women; it was well known that the woman they were here to see tonight was a lesbian.

It was Saturday night, the opening night of an Australian east coast tour by the hugely popular American rock singer, Samantha Knight.

The house lights began to dim and a hush spread throughout the auditorium. The stage was slowly suffused in pink light as the house lights were completely extinguished. Deep blue lights spilled down the backdrop in rich streaks against the pink, and a smoke effect made the scene slightly hazy. At the edges of the soft light, Julia could see the band and drums, keyboards and glinting guitars. Suddenly, a bright spotlight hit center stage and into it walked Samantha Knight.

The crowd went wild; women jumped out of their seats, screaming and cheering. Samantha opened her arms to them and just stood there smiling for a couple of minutes, as if waiting for them to settle down.

Julia had seen photos of Samantha Knight that portrayed a very attractive woman, but it was clear that none of them had done her justice. Her hair was fairly short at the sides, a little longer at the nape of her neck and longer still and fuller on top. A rich golden blond, it tumbled over her forehead in a natural, attractively tousled fashion. She had a nice tan and her skin looked radiant. She was wearing

2

tight, black wet-look pants and a matching loose jacket with casually pushed-up sleeves. The jacket was open, revealing a hot-pink, shimmering bikini-style top. She had a fabulous body, and Julia concluded she was a pretty sexy woman.

"Hello, everyone. I'm so happy to be here," Samantha said, and the crowd screamed even louder. Her voice was low and seductively throaty, with a velvety, soft Southern drawl.

A heartbeat later, the band crashed in with the introduction to their latest hit, "Take A Chance," and the show was underway.

As the concert progressed, Julia found herself enchanted by Samantha. Her voice was powerful and charged with passion. Her performance, energetic and emotional with an underlying earthy sexuality, was balanced perfectly by her warmth and humor. Sometimes Samantha played rhythm guitar while she sang, and other times, while singing a ballad, she wandered along the front of the stage directing her performance to individual adoring women.

She possessed enormous charisma and Julia wasn't surprised to see women leaving their seats and moving down toward the stage. Some were dancing in the aisles, and the security staff were kept busy peeling a few overly excited fans off the front of the stage and holding them all back. Samantha seemed to be enjoying herself, and the concert went on for a half-hour longer than was scheduled.

The offices of *The Entertainer* magazine, where Julia worked, were in Melbourne's central business district where all the major newspapers and other publications were grouped. First thing on Monday morning, Julia met with her editor, Adele Winters, to present her review of Samantha Knight. The current issue was going to press and space had been held for Julia's article.

Adele was about fifty, with black hair cut in a page boy. It was streaked with gray, but they were subtle, carefully applied, designer streaks. Her dark eyes glinted like jet, making it impossible to see into them.

Adele finished reading Julia's review, leaned back in her chair, pressed her intercom and asked her secretary to bring in some coffee. She took a drag of her cigarette. Smoking was banned in the building, and Julia remembered once being present when an officious-looking, although quivering, representative from the administration department had come to remind Adele of the rules. "Oh, bugger off," Adele had snapped with a dismissive flick of her hand, "and stop wasting my fucking time! Tell those gray, boring little shits upstairs to get a life, for Christ's sake!"

She eyed Julia through the haze of smoke. "Well, you were bloody impressed, weren't you! Did this woman do anything wrong?"

Julia smiled at Adele's laconic tone. "No. I have to say the concert was spectacular and Samantha Knight is one of the best performers I've ever seen." Their coffee arrived and Julia watched Adele spoon three heaped teaspoons of sugar into her cup. She supposed this was what kept Adele alive, since she'd never seen her eat anything and she was painfully thin. Julia sipped her coffee. "Her manager contacted you, didn't he? About getting some local publicity? I'd like to do an interview with Samantha for next month's issue."

4

"Great!" Adele said, her eyes suddenly sparkling with interest. "I wanted to see your review before I committed us to anything. Many's the time I've seen foreign recording artists come here and unexpectedly die-in-the-arse before Australian audiences. But it looks like her popularity is only going to increase, judging by your opinion."

"And I'm not the only one who was knocked out. Did you see the great reviews in *The Weekend Australian* yesterday and *The Age* this morning?"

Adele gave a little snort of contempt. "Oh, yeah, but I don't take a lot of those reviews too seriously. They're just star-fuckers, half of those hacks." Julia rolled her eyes and chuckled. Adele drank some coffee and looked thoughtful. "I can make her next month's cover girl. I'll call her manager and arrange an interview. I know they're in Melbourne until Thursday." With a flourish and a click of her expensive gold lighter, she lit another cigarette. "Maybe you could get something interesting on the lesbian angle — something that hasn't already been hashed over, that is."

Julia picked up her teaspoon and absent-mindedly stirred her coffee as she recalled the performance on Saturday night. She remembered some of the passionate lyrics of Samantha's songs, how beautiful she looked, and the subtle but unmistakable sexuality she projected to the audience. She'd driven those thousands of women out of their minds with excitement. "Yes," Julia murmured, "that could be interesting."

CHAPTER TWO

On Tuesday morning at ten o'clock, Samantha was lying on her bed in her hotel room, propped up on one elbow with *The Entertainer* open beside her. A tray containing the remnants of her breakfast was on the end of the bed and she was eating a piece of toast. Her band had performed on Sunday and Monday nights, ending the Melbourne leg of their tour, and they were taking a break to do some sightseeing for a couple of days before leaving for Sydney on Thursday.

Her manager, Danny Goldman, was pacing up and down her room. "It's a great start — just great!" he said. "This glossy's a national magazine that every other publication takes its lead from — everyone takes notice of what it has to say about any kinda major show." He was wearing a lightweight, well-cut, dark suit and a crimson shirt open at the neck. As he paced, one hand remained in his pocket, while with the other, he frequently touched and carefully stroked his perfectly smooth, black, gelled hair. "This great review means we're all set for the rest of the run. We're goddamn lucky with our timin' that this month's issue coincided with the start of the tour." He glanced at Samantha. "It's gonna mean great sales for the album over here, Sam! And I mean great!"

Samantha finished her toast and stretched languidly. "Yeah, it's great, Danny, but slow down, honey, you're making me dizzy with all your pacing."

Danny sighed loudly in exasperation and Samantha chuckled. He was always jumping around like a catfish dangling off a rod, and she was always telling him, "Slow down, honey."

"Now, don't forget you've got an interview with Julia Moran this afternoon at four-thirty. She's the one who wrote that glowin' review, and I've heard she's a heavy-weight — one of their top writers. They say a review from her can make or break a show, so you be very goddamn nice to her."

Samantha smiled and fluttered her eyelashes. "Oh, I'll be nice to her, honey, don't you worry about that."

Danny sighed again and stroked his hair in an agitated fashion. Samantha laughed. She liked teasing him; he never knew when she was joking. With a confused shake of his head, he left.

* * * * *

Promptly at four-thirty, Julia knocked on Samantha's hotel room door. When Samantha opened it she looked slightly taken aback, as if surprised to see her. Julia smiled. "You were expecting me, weren't you, Samantha? I'm Julia Moran."

Then Samantha beamed a smile at her. "Of course I am. Come in, Julia, it's lovely to meet you." They shook hands, and while Julia sat down on the sofa, got out her notes and set up her tape recorder on the coffee table, Samantha got her a glass of water and fixed a bourbon on ice for herself.

She was wearing black jeans and a white tank top. She wasn't wearing any makeup apart from a touch of mascara on her fair lashes, and she looked even more attractive than she'd looked on stage. She had that glowing kind of complexion that some blonds have, which tans easily to an even honey color. Julia noticed as Samantha brought their drinks over that she moved in a smooth, unhurried fashion with a slight roll to her hips, which was quite a contrast to her agile, energetic stage performance.

Samantha handed Julia her water and sat down on the sofa opposite her. She smiled warmly and looked directly into Julia's eyes, holding her gaze, as she said in her lilting, velvety voice, "I'm ready when you are, ma'am."

Samantha's eyes were a clear deep green. They exhibited friendliness and warmth, but Julia found her compelling gaze unsettling. She fumbled with her notes and dropped her pen on the floor. "I seem to be a bit clumsy this afternoon."

"That's okay, honey," Samantha replied softly. "There's no rush."

Julia began asking her questions. Much had been written about Samantha and she knew she was going over a lot of old ground. But she let Samantha talk, waiting for that special moment, when something interesting would come up that she could hang a story on.

Samantha was born thirty-four years ago, in Atlanta, Georgia, and had been brought up there. Her parents were killed in a car accident nearly ten years ago, and she had one sister she saw occasionally who lived in Chicago with her husband and three sons. After graduating from high school, Samantha studied music at Georgia State University part-time while she began her musical career. For seven years she worked in clubs and bars with various bands, usually as a backing singer, until she got a break with a blues band which was very popular around Atlanta at the time.

"They took me on as lead singer and that's when things really took off for me. That's also where I met Ruby eight years ago. She's very talented, you know. You'll notice from the credits on my CD liners that we work together on the arrangements of many of my songs. She played keyboards and guitar and did backing vocals with that blues band, just like she does with me now." Ice cubes tinkled as Samantha sipped her bourbon. "We took to each other straight off and she's been my closest friend ever since."

"So where'd you go from there?"

"Well, I started to meet the right people, you know, in the recording business and I did session work on various albums as a backing singer. Then after a while I started a band of my own. It was trial and error until I got my own sound together, and I had a few bands before I felt happy about where I was going."

"Is that when you started performing your own songs?"

"Yeah, I got noticed about five years ago with the bluesy kind of rock I do now. I got Ruby on board when I got my first recording contract and things have just gone on from there."

Julia was impressed with the modest, relaxed way Samantha talked about her career, under-playing her enormous success and popularity. Her first CD had been released three years ago and had flown immediately to the top of the charts in the U.S. She'd released her third CD six months ago, and before arriving in Australia for her first overseas tour, she'd just completed a three-month tour around the States.

"So, you still live in Atlanta?"

Samantha's eyes took on a faraway expression and she smiled. "Oh, no, ma'am, I live in Savannah."

Julia's pulse quickened. *Savannah.* It was a place she'd read about and that a few friends who'd been there had told her about, and in her mind it was a magical, beautiful, eccentric place that she longed to visit some day. She'd been on a couple of brief working visits to the West Coast but hadn't so far made it down to the South.

She instantly pictured Samantha writing her songs in one of those gorgeous grand old houses she'd seen in films, getting her inspiration from the landscape and the colorful characters that Julia imagined lived there. She wished she'd asked the question earlier — it was just the sort of thing she could build a story around: Samantha's lifestyle in this dreamy, steamy place edged by marshes, by the sea.

Julia glanced at her watch and was surprised to see it was close to six-thirty. They'd been talking for nearly two hours and she couldn't really expect Samantha to want to continue the interview for much longer.

Samantha stood and sauntered over to the mini-bar. Casually, over her shoulder, she said, "You haven't asked me about my sexuality — journalists always do." Samantha was smiling in good humor. "Would you like another drink?"

"Oh, no thanks." Julia wandered over to the window. It was May, nearly winter, and night was falling. The lights in the city buildings were sparkling in the twilight, and she could make out Port Philip Bay in the distance, a shimmering silvery-gray in this light. "This must be a great view in the daytime."

"Yeah, it's a spectacular view." Julia heard the clink of ice cubes and she turned to Samantha, who was sipping her drink, gazing at her. She saw Samantha's eyes flicker, almost imperceptibly, from Julia's legs and body to her eyes.

"To be honest, I was planning to ask you about that part of your life. But having met you, it seems irrelevant. I mean, what would I ask? Is being a lesbian a problem for you in your work? Obviously not. Or, when did you first realize you were gay? It doesn't really matter, does it?" She smiled. "Of course, if you had a special romance in your life that you wanted to tell me about, that'd be good for my story."

Samantha grinned and shook her head. "I'm afraid not, honey. I can't help you there."

Julia began to pack up her things. "If we had

more time, I'd really like to talk to you about your life in Savannah. It's a place that's always intrigued me."

"Have dinner with me tonight," Samantha said quickly.

Julia was surprised and hesitated for a moment.

"I'll tell you anything you wanna know about Savannah." Samantha smiled appealingly.

Julia laughed. "Well, how could I refuse an offer like that? Where would you like to go?"

"Somewhere very quiet and very relaxed. I've been away from home for so long that I'm tired of noisy restaurants. Actually, we could stay here and order room service. The food's pretty good."

Julia thought for a moment. "If you really want quiet and relaxed you could come to my place. It's only ten minutes from here, in East Melbourne, and it's a lot more comfortable than this room. I was just planning to cook something simple for myself tonight, and you're welcome to join me if you like." She grinned. "But it won't be haute cuisine, I'm afraid."

Samantha looked delighted. "That'd be great, if it's no trouble for you. I haven't been inside a home for months. I'd love that."

Julia wrote down her address. "Come over around eight o'clock. I look forward to it."

As Samantha closed the door behind Julia, she wondered why she was doing this. She had watched Julia pack up her notes and put away her tape recorder and suddenly felt, overwhelmingly, that she didn't want Julia to go. On impulse, without a thought, she had suggested dinner, and when Julia accepted, she was thrilled.

No doubt Julia would be charming and intelligent company, and she didn't mind at all telling her about Savannah. But Samantha had to admit that the real reason she'd suggested dinner was that Julia was so cute and sexy.

When she opened the door to Julia, she had found herself looking into the most exquisite eyes she'd ever seen. Throughout the interview she thought about the right word to describe their color. They seemed to change hue from blues to greens, depending on the angle, and she finally decided they were aquamarine.

She hoped Julia hadn't noticed her staring. Well, so what if she had, Samantha thought as she rummaged through her wardrobe for a sweater to wear tonight. Julia seemed uneasy at first but she soon relaxed. Samantha pictured her sitting with her gorgeous legs crossed, sipping her drink and looking attentive as she answered the questions. Samantha found she often had to glance away from Julia to maintain her concentration.

She's almost certainly straight, Samantha thought, and anyway, straight or not, she'd never see her again after tonight. For God's sake, it wasn't even an issue. She was just having dinner with a nice woman who shared her passion for Savannah.

She opened a packet of macadamia nuts she found in the bar fridge and turned on the TV to catch the news. But all the while, in the back of her mind, she could see Julia in her sophisticated, well-cut business suit and high heels, walking over to the window. She had such a confident, elegant stride. The skirt was short and her legs were long and when she turned to Samantha, with a toss of her chestnut-brown hair, Samantha's heart had skipped a beat.

CHAPTER THREE

Samantha paid the taxi driver and looked up at the large, two-story Victorian house. Glancing along the street she could see that all of the houses were similar and equally well-kept. On the opposite side of the road was a large tree-filled park. She opened the dark green iron gate and walked up the bluestone steps to the wide, lace-fringed veranda.

Julia opened the door with a bright smile and invited Samantha into the entrance hall. The house was warm and the music of Jevetta Steele was beating gently in the background. Looking relaxed, Julia was holding a glass of red wine. She had changed into faded jeans, a cream-colored V-neck sweater of fine wool and cream woolen socks, and she still managed to look glamorous. She was more than medium height, but without her high heels not quite as tall as Samantha.

Suddenly a black and white, splotchy-patterned cat bounded down the hallway to Samantha and began rubbing around her legs. "That's Magpie," Julia said as Samantha bent down to stroke its head. "She loves visitors."

Samantha glanced around. The hallway ahead of them was long, with doors off to either side, and the floors were dark, highly polished hardwood. An Oriental carpet ran down the center of the hall. Ahead of them, to the right of the hall, was a carved timber staircase. "This is a lovely house," she said.

"Thanks, I'll show you around. There's not much to see upstairs, just three bedrooms and the bathrooms."

The study to the right had bookcases built on either side of a black marble fireplace. A large antique oak desk with a computer on it sat under the window that overlooked the front garden and park.

Samantha noticed a photo of a middle-aged couple on the mantelpiece. The woman was good-looking and resembled Julia. "Are these your parents?"

"Yes. They live in South Australia now. When my father retired they moved there and bought a small vineyard." Julia chuckled. "It was always their dream, but I think Dad's discovered it's a lot more work than he expected. Still, they have a good life there and it's a great place to go for a visit."

"Do you have any brothers or sisters?"

"No, there's only me."

The sitting room was on the other side of the hall and furnished with a deep-rose-colored sofa and two matching high-backed chairs. A beautiful, classic Japanese cabinet dominated one wall, and two huge Japanese vases stood on either side of the hearth.

The last door along the hall opened into the dining room. A cherrywood table that could seat ten stood in the center of the room, the chairs upholstered in the same deep-rose fabric. A chaise lounge nestled against one wall, piled with cushions. Samantha glanced up at the ornate chandelier, at odds, she thought, with the rest of the decor.

Julia laughed. "It's a bit over the top, I know. It was here when I bought the place and I planned to get rid of it, but by the time I got around to decorating this room, I'd sort of grown used to it. I imagine some previous owner, perhaps during the Forties, lovingly choosing it and going to a lot of trouble to hang it. It was probably expensive and they would've thought it was absolutely beautiful." She shrugged. "It *is* quite beautiful, really. It's just in the wrong place. Maybe that's what appeals to me. Anyway, now it's got a dimmer on it, and at dinner parties, when it's set very low, it's magical the way it glitters." She grinned. "Well, after a few drinks, it seems that way."

Samantha smiled. "I think it's great. How long have you been here?" Julia led her out of the hall, then turned left into the kitchen. It was well designed and functional, with travertine bench tops and stainless steel appliances.

"Five years. I had a lot to do to the place. It was a bit of a mess when I bought it. But I've finished now, thank God. I bought it right after my divorce. I wanted to set myself up comfortably and securely on my own, because I imagine I'll stay single — it suits me. What can I get you to drink?"

"Well . . . bourbon would be nice if you have it, but otherwise wine's okay."

Julia tossed her hair. "I bought some bourbon for you on the way home. I knew you'd want that."

Samantha smiled. "That was nice. Thank you." As Julia got the ice and poured her drink, Samantha couldn't help but notice the way her jeans hugged her firm hips and the thin sweater showed off the shape of her full breasts. She wondered why this gorgeous woman saw herself as being single all her life. "So you're not in any kind of relationship then?"

"Well, yes, I am, I guess. But it's fairly casual with Ben. He's away a lot and I go away fairly often, so I don't see him all the time, which is just fine." She drank some wine. "I'd better start cooking. I hope you like lamb. I'm pan-frying some lamb fillets to have with new potatoes and salad."

"Sounds great. Can I do anything? Not that I'm much use in a kitchen," Samantha said with a shrug.

"No, it won't take long." Julia placed the fillets onto a cast iron skillet and drizzled a small amount of olive oil over the top, a squeeze of lemon juice, some crushed garlic and some fresh oregano. The sizzling sound and delicious aroma soon filled the kitchen. She did it all in a relaxed, organized way.

Samantha sipped her bourbon. It felt good just being there, leaning against the bench watching her. Julia had already made her feel completely at home so she didn't feel at all like a visitor in a stranger's house.

Julia checked on the potatoes, then turned to Samantha. She sipped her wine. "Tomorrow's your last day in Melbourne. What are you planning to do?"

"Ruby and I are going shopping. The others are planning a drive down to Apollo Bay along The Great Ocean Road. Is that what it's called?"

"Yes. It's a pity you're not going with them. It's incredibly beautiful down there. It's on some kind of registry as one of the most scenic drives in the world."

Samantha frowned. "Yeah, but we've been told Melbourne's good for shopping and if I don't go shopping with Ruby tomorrow, she'll kill me. She's a shopaholic, that woman."

Julia chuckled. "Well, remind me before you leave tonight to write you a list of the best areas to go. You don't want to bother with the department stores in the city. All the best, interesting shops and restaurants are hidden around the inner suburbs. You might find something a little different. Melbourne doesn't make things easy for tourists. You have to know where to go."

"That'd be great," Samantha said with a smile. "Ruby'll be delighted."

The music finished and Samantha offered to put on something else. Julia led her into the modern, open-plan living room that was off the kitchen. The floor here was also polished hardwood with large Oriental rugs scattered around. There were three comfortable-looking sofas and a low coffee table. The room looked out through a wall of glass doors onto a small, leafy, brick-paved garden.

"The CD's are in here," Julia said, opening a large Victorian sideboard. There was a huge selection and they were carefully categorized. Samantha's eyes widened at the sight. Julia shrugged. "I have to keep up with everything that comes out. People send me things and a lot of what's there is crap. I'd better get back to the stove."

Samantha noticed on top of the sideboard a stack of back issues of *The Entertainer*. "Do you mind if I take a look through some of these?"

"Not at all. Sit down and relax. Dinner won't be long." Julia went back to the kitchen.

Samantha selected some Beethoven piano sonatas and sat on a sofa with a few magazines. Magpie jumped onto her lap and curled up into a ball.

Fifteen minutes later, Julia returned with a bowl of salad, plates and cutlery. "I thought we'd eat in here — the dining room's awfully formal for two." She grinned. "I have to say, I'm a little surprised at your choice of music."

"Oh, well, there's more to life than rock and roll, honey."

Julia laughed, and Samantha noticed how her eyes sparkled and her whole face seemed to light up.

"I see Magpie's taken a particular liking to you," Julia said. She squatted down beside Samantha's knees and rubbed her head against Magpie's. "You're such a cheeky cat." Julia's hair hung just past her shoulders and it brushed over Samantha's hand. She smiled up at her. "She just assumes everyone's going to adore her and want her fur all over their clothes."

Julia's perfume was a soft, seductive fragrance and her close proximity made Samantha tingle. "You've got the most beautiful eyes I've ever seen." The words were barely out of her mouth before she regretted them.

As if stunned, Julia held her gaze for a moment longer, then looked away and stood up. "Thank you," she said evenly. "I'll just go and bring in the rest of the food." She walked out to the kitchen.

Shit! Samantha thought. Julia probably thought she was trying to hit on her or something. Embarrassed, she followed Julia. "I'll help you."

"Thanks. You could open the wine and bring the glasses."

She was relieved that Julia seemed fine. "That looks great," Samantha said, watching Julia slice the fillets into small, pink rounds and arrange them on a plate.

They returned to the living room and were soon settled on opposite sofas with their plates of food on their laps.

Julia sipped her wine and looked at Samantha with a smile. "So, Savannah. I assume you've read *Midnight in the Garden of Good and Evil*. Is the place really that wonderful?"

"Oh, yeah, that was a great book. John Berendt really captured the spirit of Savannah. It's full of weird characters." She grinned. "But the downside for some of us is the increase in tourists since his book came out. It's teeming with them on weekends." She paused, suddenly missing home and her friends. She wondered what they'd all been doing, what had changed. "I vaguely remember going there for a passing visit when I was a child, but I didn't see it again until about six years ago. Friends of mine had moved there — Donna and Candice — and I thought, why in God's name would they wanna live in a little town like that? But when I visited them, I just fell in love with the place, and I bought a house there three and a half years ago."

Julia's eyes were bright and attentive. She tossed her hair back over her shoulder. "Tell me about your house."

"Well there's a section of the city that's the National Landmark District. There are heaps of gorgeous old mansions in that area that've been completely restored. They're eighteenth- and nineteenth-century buildings. My house is just outside that area, close to the Savannah River. I'm also fairly close to the wharf. All the old warehouses have been turned into galleries, restaurants and shops. It was once an important seaport where they exported cotton. My house is typical Savannah Victorian. It's painted white and it's pretty big — too big, really, for just me. But I couldn't resist the wide, sweeping staircase that spirals up from the center of the entrance hall. It dominates the house and it's quite spectacular."

"God," Julia breathed. "Does it have shutters on the windows?"

Samantha smiled at Julia's dreamy-eyed expression. "Yes, ma'am, it sure does. The place still needs some repairs and redecorating, though. I got the kitchen and bathrooms remodeled, and landscaped the garden, but I haven't got around to doing a lot of other things. Actually, I should get some advice from you. You've done a great job with this place."

Julia rolled her eyes. "I'd think I'd died and gone to heaven, working on a house like that." She emptied the bottle into their glasses. "What about the people? I've always imagined it would have a small-town kind of attitude that could make things uncomfortable for a rock star — especially a gay one."

"It's a unique place. It has aspects of that small-town thing, but with worldly airs and graces too. Everyone seems to gossip about everyone else but they don't ever seem to judge people." Samantha chuckled, remembering Doris and Walter. "I've got this elderly couple who live next door to me, and they drop in occasionally for a drink in the afternoons. They're always full of stories about everyone, and I'm sure they go and repeat anything I tell them. But they don't criticize — no one does. On the contrary, they seem grateful for all the things the locals get up to, if only for the entertainment value." Smiling to herself, she pictured Walter and Doris on fine Sunday afternoons, cruising slowly around town in their 1972 Rolls Royce Corniche convertible, waving and yelling out, "Lovely day, ain't it," to everybody they passed.

Julia leaned forward to pick up her glass from the table, and Samantha caught a tantalizing glimpse of her cleavage. "I had an affair with a woman there a year ago, and I thought we were being extremely discreet. But it turns out that everybody knew all about it, all along." She shrugged. "They just loved it."

They both laughed. Julia got up and put on some more music — Mozart Piano Concertos. "I'll get another bottle of wine," she said, as she headed out to the kitchen with the dishes.

Samantha tried not to think about her great body and the sexy way she walked.

Julia poured more wine, then sat down and looked at Samantha with a hint of a smile. "So what happened with her? Didn't it work out?"

Samantha found herself gazing at Julia again, mesmerized, like an idiot. Julia's eyes were fringed with long, thick lashes, and she had a way of looking at Samantha that was demure and provocative at the same time. It's not her fault, she thought. She can't help having bedroom eyes.

Samantha shook her head dismissively. "No, it most certainly didn't work out." The last thing she wanted to talk about was Elizabeth. "Anyway, that's enough about me. I noticed in one of those magazines some photos and a story about an award presentation for journalists. Looks like you've won quite a few. I was impressed. How long have you been writing for *The Entertainer*?"

"About eight years —" The phone rang, interrupting her. The machine cut straight in and Julia waited to hear who was calling.

"Hi, darling," said a male voice, "I just got back from Perth . . . You're obviously not home . . . I'll call you tomorrow. Love you."

Samantha was surprised that Julia made no move to answer the phone and was frowning slightly as she picked up her glass and took a large gulp. "I assume that was Ben. You didn't wanna talk to him?"

Julia tossed her hair and leaned back on the sofa. "I can call him tomorrow."

Samantha knew she shouldn't keep asking personal questions, but she couldn't resist. Julia fascinated her. "You said your relationship was casual, but he sounded pretty serious. He said he loved you."

Julia sighed. "Yes, I think perhaps he does. I don't feel that way, though, but then, I never do."

Samantha's curiosity rapidly increased. "What do you mean?"

Julia sipped her wine and looked thoughtful. She didn't seem to mind the questions. "It used to bother me, but I don't think about it much these days. My relationships never seem to work out all that well. I think it'd be great to have a relationship where I feel really close . . . you know, intimate with a guy, and feel like I've got an equal partner to share everything with. Women friends of mine seem to be able to achieve that — to a point." She laughed softly. "I think they often put up with a lot of shit, myself, but they still seem to find more happiness than I do." She looked directly at Samantha with a slightly troubled expression. "Men always seem to be on another wavelength, and whenever I try to talk about my feelings or aspirations, they become confused or competitive or threatened. It makes me withdraw emotionally. I don't know how other women deal with it." She curled up on the sofa.

"Yeah, I don't know how women figure them out. They're from another planet as far as I'm concerned," Samantha said with a grin.

Julia laughed. "Yeah, well, I got married ten years ago when I was only twenty-three. He was a nice guy and I really cared about him, but I wasn't in love — there was no passion, and for me he was more like a friend. It's no surprise it only lasted five years and most of that was difficult. It's the same with Ben, except that now I know not to expect too much. I've decided to be satisfied with a comfortable arrangement, where I live my own life and, if possible, have a lover to enjoy some nice times with." She shrugged. "Ben's a great guy, but when he's around too much I often just want to run away from him." She smiled. "That sounds terrible, doesn't it?"

While she listened to Julia talk, Samantha observed the expression of hurt and disappointment in her eyes, and something turned over inside her. Her attraction to Julia took on another dimension. It was no longer simply an admiration for her beauty, but a powerful desire for the woman herself. It was inappropriate, she chided herself, and she didn't want it, but there it was. She swallowed and smiled weakly. "You've never fallen in love?"

Julia looked candidly into Samantha's eyes and shook her head. "I guess I'm just not the type."

Oh, honey, you're most definitely the type. Samantha felt a sudden urge to take Julia in her arms, and desire rippled through her body at the thought. She swallowed some wine. "You just haven't met the right person yet."

"Perhaps not," Julia said lightly. "Would you like some coffee?"

"Yeah, that'd be great." Samantha was glad to change the subject. She went with Julia to the kitchen. "There's something I wanna ask you, Julia, that occurred to me earlier. About your doing a feature on my band."

Julia boiled water for the coffee plunger. "Sounds interesting."

"Well, when I was skimming through your magazines, I came across the feature you wrote about a British blues band. It was wonderful the way you wrote about them, their aspirations and the style of their music and everything. Their personalities really came through. I was thinking you could cover the rest of our tour, you know, travel with us and write about all of us and the concerts, you know the sort of thing."

Julia ran her hand through her hair. "How long is the rest of your tour?"

"There's about ten days left of a two-week tour. We've got three performances in both Sydney and Brisbane, with a few days off in between to look around. We toured so hard in the States that I wanted this one to be nice and easy — give everyone a bit of a break at the same time." Samantha grinned. "You wouldn't be rushing around. There'd be lots of time to talk with everyone and have some fun too."

Julia poured the coffee and they carried their cups back into the living room. "Well, it's perfect timing for it to be in the next issue. That's when today's interview is planned to appear."

Samantha smiled. "This'd be much better than that little interview."

Julia nodded, enthusiastically. "The schedule would be tight, but I think it'd be really good. There's nothing big happening in town over the next couple of weeks that I'd have to cover, and I wouldn't get an argument from my editor about doing a feature on Samantha Knight." She grinned. "You're hot property at the moment. But wouldn't you need to discuss this with your manager?"

"Oh, we don't need to worry about Danny. He'll think it's a great idea. He loves publicity more than anything."

"*Good* publicity, you mean."

"Well, he prefers good publicity, but if stretched,

27

he'd settle for bad. He's always telling me, 'You gotta have 'em talkin' about you, Sam. When they stop talkin', you're dead! I mean it — finished!' " They both laughed.

"Okay, let me talk to my editor about it in the morning and I'll get back to you."

Their conversation turned to other subjects for an hour or so, then Samantha glanced at her watch. It was just past midnight. "I'd better be going. Thanks a lot for tonight. I've really enjoyed it."

"Me too," Julia said. "I'll call you a taxi and I'll write out that list of shopping places I mentioned."

"Great. Ruby's gonna be very excited. Let me write my address in Savannah for you, while I think of it. Just in case you can't make it on the tour, you be sure to phone me when you're in my part of the world."

"Oh, I definitely will. Thanks." They exchanged notes, and Samantha heard the taxi beeping outside as Julia showed her to the door. "Goodnight, Samantha. I'll talk to you tomorrow." She kissed Samantha's cheek.

Samantha felt another melting ripple. It would be so easy to slip her arm around Julia's waist and kiss that luscious-looking mouth. She smiled. "Goodnight, and thanks again."

On the way back to her hotel, Samantha worried about her feelings for Julia. It was ridiculous to indulge herself with this attraction. But if she was honest, this was the main reason she had suggested Julia travel with them and do the feature story. Of course, it would be good for the band, she told herself. Julia was a top writer with a prestigious magazine.

But more than anything, it was an excuse to spend more time with her.

Thank God, Julia's straight, she thought. If she wasn't, and happened to show any interest in Samantha, things would get complicated. She couldn't get involved in some affair that would be over in ten days — not with a woman like Julia. She remembered the way Julia had looked at her at times, and how it made her think twice. No, she was straight. And she'd better make sure that Julia remained unaware of Samantha's attraction for her.

As the taxi pulled up outside the hotel, Samantha sighed. She loved Julia's habit of tossing back her hair — it was so sexy, that insouciant little toss of her head. God, she thought, a woman could drown in those eyes, if she wasn't real careful.

CHAPTER FOUR

Julia cleaned up the kitchen and got ready for bed. She liked Samantha a lot, but there was another intriguing layer to her that was different from other women she liked. The looks Samantha gave her were subtle and flattering. There was also some degree of sexual overtone in the way Samantha reacted to her, but it was benign, comfortable, and nothing like the looks or reactions she got from men, which made her uneasy. Samantha was very much a woman, with all the qualities that Julia liked about women. They were usually warmer, more thoughtful and compassionate than men, in Julia's experience, and usually more fun too. It was interesting, she thought, that she'd always preferred the company of women.

Julia had only just met her, but she felt completely comfortable talking to Samantha about her relationships. Samantha seemed genuinely interested in what she was saying, as if Julia's feelings mattered to her. She had a delightful way of making Julia feel she was the most important person in the world. She'd be like that with everyone, Julia supposed. It was part of her charm and charisma.

She got into bed and lay there thinking about her friends. She had never even discussed her feelings about men with them the way she had with Samantha. Her friends always teased her, saying she was way too fussy in her expectations and that was why she wasn't in a serious, stable relationship. It was easier to laugh and agree with them than try to explain things she knew they wouldn't understand.

There were four women, two of whom she'd met at university. She saw them quite regularly, for lunches and occasional dinners or shows when their partners were busy or away. They were good fun to be with and held demanding careers like her own, but their lovers or husbands were their first priority, and Julia couldn't empathize with their feelings emotionally or sexually for men. She was the only one who hadn't fallen madly and passionately in love at some time.

It made sense, she thought, that Samantha would understand her, when she knew her friends could not.

Smiling, she pictured Samantha, her blond hair tumbling over her forehead, that attractive habit of absent-mindedly twirling a lock of hair in her fingers.

She decided to phone Adele early tomorrow and

arrange a breakfast meeting with her to discuss the feature. She hoped she'd be able to go on the tour. It would be a lot of fun, and Julia imagined she and Samantha would become great friends.

At eight-thirty the next morning, Julia and Adele were sitting in a city restaurant, a block from their office. Julia was eating a cheese and tomato omelet with mushrooms on the side, and buttered toast.

Adele finished her short black coffee and lit another cigarette. She visibly shuddered at the sight of Julia's breakfast. "God, how can you eat like that first thing in the morning?"

Julia grinned. "Because I'm starving. Don't you ever eat?"

"Not if I can bloody avoid it. Now tell me all about this feature you have in mind."

Julia explained how Samantha had come up with the idea after looking through some issues of the magazine, and how she seemed really keen to do it. "So, what do you think?"

"Frankly, I can't believe our luck. You must've really impressed her. She doesn't have any problem getting the publicity she wants. She'd have major publications everywhere asking to do features like this. She can pick and choose."

Julia finished her coffee and looked at Adele with an amused smile. "So, she's fussy. She wants the best. And it won't hurt her album sales in Australia one bit."

Adele waved over the waiter and ordered them both more coffee. "Yeah, well, whatever the reason, the advertising director's going to owe me after this. She's going to have the whole month to sign up some big spenders who'll want to be on those pages." She drew deeply on her cigarette and coughed. "I was holding half a page for your interview, but I'll make it at least four pages now, allowing for plenty of photos."

"So, I've got the go-ahead to leave with them tomorrow?"

"I'll have to talk to her manager. He might have some stipulations of some sort," said Adele. "But otherwise, it's fine by me."

Julia pushed aside her empty plate and sipped her coffee. "I'll need to take a photographer, of course, and I was thinking this morning about Kerry Oliver."

"Kerry's only a junior. I think this job's too big for her. Someone more experienced would be better," said Adele. "Did you think of her because she's gay, by any chance?"

"I've worked with her on enough jobs to know she'd be right for this. She uses light well and I like the way she looks at things. The fact that she's gay, and more than likely a big fan, wouldn't hurt, would it?"

Adele looked doubtful. "There are more senior photographers who'd murder me if I sent Kerry on a job like this."

Julia looked at her directly. "She's who I want, Adele." Julia knew Adele could be difficult, but if she was firm enough with her, she would get what she wanted.

Adele lit another cigarette and seemed to hide behind the haze. "I'll see what I can do. You'll have to let me know within a few days, your plans for the story — what issues you're going to cover and that kind of thing, so we can plan the space and Miranda can target the right advertisers." She looked off into the distance for a moment. "I wonder if they've got any airline deals or something. The ad department should call their promotions company and find out."

Julia laughed and shook her head in exasperation. "God, Adele, I wouldn't have any idea. But I can tell you this. I see the whole article being very female — feminine, I suppose. This band is female driven, devoid of any male influence, and Samantha's music is directed to women. I want to capture the quintessential Samantha Knight. So, don't ask me to sneak in stuff like 'Samantha Knight's band is flying with Qantas Airlines' or any shit like that, okay?"

Adele looked unmoved. She shrugged. "It wouldn't hurt to work in something like that." She grinned. "Especially if Miranda can organize a nice bit of contra she can share with us."

Julia was well aware that Adele was a good editor. She knew a good story when she saw one, but was seldom inspired in advance. She always had her mind on the broader picture of the magazine's financial success and didn't mind sharing in the odd windfall that was a normal and more or less above-board part of life in the advertising department. She often pushed for subtle marketing messages to be included in the copy — ads in disguise.

Julia shook her head. "Not on this one, Adele. This is going to be good — I can feel it. I'm not playing any games with the ad department."

Adele's black eyes held Julia's gaze for a moment, as if trying to stare Julia into submission. Julia had seen it all before and just smiled. Adele sniffed, then she signed the credit card receipt and they left for the office.

Julia closed her office door and thought she really should call Ben. She felt guilty about not phoning him first thing this morning. He had, after all, been away working for three weeks.

It occurred to her, as it had often before, that she really wasn't very fair to him. On her list of life's priorities, Ben was near the bottom. There were times during his frequent absences when Julia thought she needed him and looked forward to his return, but she'd long ago grown accustomed to a feeling of unexplained disappointment when they were reunited. She could still feel desperately lonely when she was in his arms.

When she awoke this morning, her thoughts were filled with the project she'd planned with Samantha, not Ben.

There was a knock at her door and as she looked up, Ben walked in. "Hello, gorgeous," he said with a beaming smile.

"I was just going to phone you." Julia went to him. He wrapped her in his arms and held her tightly.

"I've missed you," he said. He kissed her mouth hard with an urgent need, like he always did, as if searching for something in Julia that he couldn't find.

Her phone rang and she moved to answer it, but Ben held onto her. "Forget the phone," he murmured and began to kiss her again. She felt his sexual arousal swelling against her body and she pulled back slightly. It irritated her that he couldn't just hug her affectionately without always getting turned on.

Then her intercom buzzed and her assistant, Tracy, announced, "Julia, Samantha Knight's on line one."

Julia pulled away from Ben quickly and grabbed the phone. "Hi, Samantha, how are you?"

"Fine, honey. It seems you're coming with us tomorrow." She gave her low throaty chuckle. "I just had Danny in here carrying on. Your editor got on to him before I had a chance to tell him our plans. You should have heard him!" She laughed again.

"Sorry about that. Is he okay about everything?"

"Oh, he's fine. He loves the idea. Listen, why don't you and I have dinner again tonight. I'd like to take you somewhere nice to repay your hospitality."

"You don't need to do that."

"I'd like to. We can talk about your plans for the story, if you're free. A Chinese place would be great, if you like Chinese food."

Julia laughed too. Samantha's charm was very persuasive. "I do, and I know just the place. I'll book a table."

"Great. Come to the hotel around seven-thirty and I'll introduce you to everyone. We'll be in Danny's room having a drink. Room three-oh-three. 'Bye, honey."

Julia turned to Ben, who was looking somewhat dejected. "Must've been a very important call," he said flatly.

"Oh, yeah, I'm sorry, but you know how it is. Business is business." She smiled as sweetly as she could. *He's not going to like this.* "I'm having dinner with Samantha tonight. It's important that we discuss a feature that I'm writing about her."

Ben looked angry. "You knew I was going to be home, why'd you organize a working dinner tonight?"

Julia felt another pang of guilt. It wasn't really necessary to have dinner with Samantha tonight — they'd have plenty of time to discuss the feature later. But she was excited about the tour, and it would be helpful to meet Danny Goldman and the band members before they all set off together.

"I'm sorry, Ben. I didn't know about all this until yesterday. It's just the way things have turned out — bad timing. And that's not all. I'll be leaving tomorrow for Sydney and Brisbane, touring with Samantha and her band. I'll be gone for about ten days."

Ben looked like he was getting ready for an argument. He allowed nothing to stand in the way of his own business obligations or opportunities, she thought, but always became petulant when she did the same thing.

"Maybe we could meet in Noosa Heads or Port Douglas for a few days together after my job's finished. That'd be nice, wouldn't it?" She smiled, hoping he'd be mollified.

Ben gave a defeated shrug. "Yeah, I guess so. I'll see if I can get some time off." He walked over to her and held her again. "Samantha Knight. She's a dyke, isn't she? She'd better keep her hands off you." He chuckled. "You'd better watch yourself, sweetheart."

Julia felt a rush of anger. "She's a woman, not a man." She knew she sounded terse. "With several million lesbians around the world who adore her, I don't think Samantha would have to bother groping straight women, do you?"

"Okay, okay, I was only kidding. Now, if it was a great-looking guy you were traveling with, I might really be worried."

Julia wasn't pacified. She wondered whether it was his possessiveness that aggravated her, or the suggestion that only the potent threat from a male was worth taking seriously. He probably thought the alternative was some kind of joke.

She covered her irritation with a smile. "I've got a lot to organize, Ben. I'm leaving in the morning. I'll fax you a copy of my itinerary and we'll talk in a couple of days, okay?"

He kissed her again and promised to call. They said goodbye and he left for his office.

Her phone rang. It was Adele. "It's all set, Julia. You'll be going on the tour. Danny Goldman seems very pleased about it all. I've got Kerry for you like you wanted, but there are senior photographers who'll want to skin me alive for this. Her pictures will need to be fantastic! I got a fax of the itinerary from Danny and I've sent a copy around to Tracy. Make sure she's booking everything for you." As usual, Adele was going at a million miles an hour.

"Okay, I'll do some planning on the feature and come and see you later today."

Julia left work a little early so she could pick up Magpie and take her to her usual cattery. Gum Nut was Magpie's home away from home, as Julia traveled frequently, and it was a comfort to know the couple who ran the place spoiled her. Magpie always came home relaxed and happy. Then Julia hurried back home to shower and change before heading off to Samantha's hotel on Southbank, beside the Yarra River in the heart of the city.

CHAPTER FIVE

Julia knocked on Danny Goldman's door and she was aware of a feeling of nervous excitement. She wasn't sure why. A moment later the door opened, and she found herself looking into Samantha's green eyes. Samantha had a way of gazing at her, as if looking right inside her, that yesterday had felt disconcerting but didn't today.

"Hi," Julia said with a grin. "Aren't you going to ask me in?"

With a throaty chuckle Samantha kissed her cheek. "Hi, Julia, come and meet everyone."

Samantha was dressed in tight black leather pants and a matching fitted sleeveless vest that just met the waistband of her pants and zipped up the front. Clearly, the outfit was made of the finest, soft leather and beautifully cut. She had the perfect body for it and she looked fabulous.

"I want y'all to meet Julia Moran," Samantha announced. "This is Danny Goldman."

Danny shook Julia's hand warmly and, with his free hand, stroked his seal-sleek hair. "This is gonna be great, Julia, just great!" he said, beaming.

"This is Don, our drummer," Samantha said. He was tall with a bleached white crew-cut and a friendly grin. "This is Louis, our bass guitarist, and Jenny, who does lead and rhythm guitars."

They had been gazing at each other adoringly until they were introduced. They let go of each other long enough to shake hands with her. Louis had an intricate pattern shaved through his cropped black hair. Jenny's brown hair went down past her waist and was streaked with blond. They both sported numerous studs in their ears, and tiny rings glittered from their eyebrows.

Samantha introduced Ruby, an attractive woman with rich, dark skin. She took Julia's hand and gazed with disarming candor into Julia's eyes. She gave a charming smile, and her dark eyes seemed to sparkle with mischief. Her straightened black hair was long and streaked subtly with auburn shades. She was dressed in layers of bright colors — a yellow cotton vest over a red T-shirt, topped with a deep green and blue loose cotton jacket. Dozens of bracelets and bangles she wore on both arms created a symphony when she moved. "Welcome aboard, honey," Ruby said, her accent stronger than Samantha's, then she kissed both Julia's cheeks.

Lisa, from Big Gig International, the tour promoters, was tall and heavily built, without being overweight. Her short, dark hair showed glimpses of gray at the temples and when she smiled, laugh lines crinkled attractively at the corners of her bright, blue eyes. As she took Julia's hand, she somehow placed herself between Samantha and Julia, causing Samantha to have to move out of the way. The hand that held Julia's was broad and strong, and she eyed Julia intently.

Julia caught Samantha's hostile glare at Lisa's indifferent profile, followed by a glance at Ruby. With a roll of her eyes, Ruby erupted into throaty giggles. "Oh, my, ain't we gonna have some fun," she drawled in the background.

"I'm delighted to meet you," said Lisa. "I've admired your work for a long time. I'm looking forward to spending some time talking with you while we're on tour."

"Thank you," Julia said. "I'm sure it's going to be very interesting."

"But right now," Samantha said with a sparkling smile, "Julia and I have a dinner date, so will you excuse us, Lisa?" She took Julia's arm and led her toward the door. She slipped on a knee-length cream linen coat and leaned close to Julia. Julia was aware of her attractive, subtle, spicy perfume. "You are ready to go, aren't you." It was a statement, not a question, and they left.

* * * * *

As they stepped outside the hotel, Samantha asked, "So, where am I taking you, ma'am?"

"The restaurant I booked is only five minutes away by taxi, but it's a mild night, we could walk if you like."

A large group of women, perhaps close to one hundred, which Julia had seen on the way in, suddenly came to life and surged toward the entrance, calling out to Samantha. Samantha smiled and waved at them. "I don't think we'll be walking, honey." She opened the door of the closest taxi and gestured for Julia to get in. "Quick, let's go," Samantha said to the driver, and they sped off.

"I thought they were a tour group," Julia said.

Samantha grinned. "They always find out where we are in five minutes. They've been outside the hotel since we arrived. It's really nice but I can't always stop to talk. I recognize some of those faces. I signed autographs for them this morning."

The restaurant was in China Town, in the city center. It had an excellent reputation for food and service, and Julia liked it because it offered cuisine from various Chinese provinces.

"Ms. Moran," said the head waiter, "it's lovely to see you again." He looked at Samantha and beamed a delighted smile of recognition. "Good evening, madam."

He showed them to a nice corner table for two, and with a flourish, shook the white starched napkins and draped them across their laps. Chinese music was playing discreetly in the background and waiters moved about quietly and efficiently. The walls were hung with heavy, ornate, lacquered Chinese screens, and the lighting was warm and intimate.

Samantha was looking at the wine list. "Would this Victorian Marsanne be good?"

Julia raised her eyebrows in surprise. "Yes, it's very good. I don't know many people who particularly like Marsanne."

Samantha gave a little half-smile. "Oh, I like lots of things, honey."

"Everyone in your band seems very nice, Danny too. I think I'm especially going to like Ruby. She looks like a woman with a sense of humor."

Samantha laughed. "Oh, she's just wonderful. You'll definitely get on well with her."

Julia recalled the way Ruby had appraised her in a frank, warm manner, and the interaction between Ruby, Samantha and Lisa. Lisa had been mildly flirtatious. "Is Ruby gay?"

"Oh, yes, ma'am. She sure is. And so is Lisa."

"And so is the photographer I'm taking with me," Julia said, smiling.

Samantha chuckled. "Well, you're gonna be surrounded by dykes, honey, I hope you can cope with us all."

"Oh, I think I'll manage," Julia murmured. She sipped her wine. Samantha was looking at her with that particular intensity again. Her eyes showed intelligence and seemed to be trying to read her. She was biting on the side of her lower lip. She didn't wear lipstick, but her full and perfectly shaped lips were a healthy-looking light pink. Like biting into a plump, ripe peach, Julia thought. "Apart from Ruby, have the other band members been with you long? They look very young."

Samantha nodded. "About a year now. They're all very talented musicians and they're only in their early twenties. It's good to keep the same players if it's all working well, but musicians can be very difficult — they come and go. I doubt that they'll all still be with me in a year's time, but it doesn't really matter. Good musicians adapt quickly when they join a band." She paused. "Louis and Jenny have fallen in love since the tour began in the States. As long as that lasts I don't imagine any problems. I'd never wanna be without Ruby though."

A waiter brought their first course of quail Sung Choi Bao, pan-fried Shanghai dumplings and West Australian scallops with ginger. The waiter, an attractive young woman in a white shirt, black bow-tie, black pants and cummerbund, give Samantha a very sweet smile as she served the food.

"This looks great," Samantha said.

Julia tasted a scallop. "Mmm, the food's always good here." She drank some wine. "I've given some thought to our feature story."

Samantha nodded as she slipped off her coat, which the waiter whisked away. Julia admired the firm, shapely muscles of her shoulders.

"Well, I want to write the whole thing from your perspective. I thought I'd get background stuff about everyone else and then write about their roles, including relevant and interesting aspects of their backgrounds, from your point of view. That way, I can work in your expectations, plans, style and future direction."

Samantha nodded again. "Sounds great."

"Everyone around you obviously has an influence on you in various ways and I want you to express that influence. It's got to be totally a Samantha Knight story."

"But you won't play down how important Ruby is to our sound or how good Danny is at running things?" Samantha picked up some food in her chopsticks. Her nails were unpainted and short, perfectly manicured.

Julia smiled. "It'll be your story, so you'll make it clear how important they are to you in the success of your band. As we go along, I'll get your reactions to the fans and venues and include aspects of traveling, so it feels like we're moving."

Samantha's expression indicated that she liked her idea. She was listening with great concentration and twirling that lock of golden hair in her fingers. Sometimes her gaze lingered on Julia's mouth.

"And I'll work in material about your process of song-writing, what inspires you, and weave the song ideas, as well as selected lyrics, in and out of the story." She paused and drank some wine. "Of course, in those parts I'd like to include glimpses of Savannah and your life there."

"I think you're very clever." Samantha's eyes were sparkling and Julia noticed again what a beautiful smile she had. It was quite captivating.

"I'm glad you think so." Julia didn't want to look away. Then the waiter arrived with their main course of Peking duck. They watched while she quickly but delicately placed the thin strips of spring onion and cucumber onto the small light pancakes, added the golden, crispy duck and sauce, and rolled them up neatly. They ordered another bottle of wine and their conversation turned to other matters.

* * * * *

Later, Julia was having trouble getting to sleep. She kept thinking about Samantha and her confusing reactions to her. Outside the hotel, Samantha's fans seemed to have disappeared for the time being. She touched Samantha's arm and moved to kiss her cheek. Samantha went to do the same thing and miscalculated. Their lips touched, and Samantha softly gasped. Julia didn't say anything. Samantha had managed a friendly smile and they said good-night. Julia noticed every little thing about her, even the way she touched her hair, for God's sake. She remembered her hands exactly, the rings she wore and the lovely shape of her straight shoulders and the muscles in her arms. And her low, husky voice. Sometimes when she spoke softly, it reminded Julia of the feel of silk sliding across her skin. Samantha had another kind of smile, too, apart from her usual friendly smile. It was a half-smile that formed slowly while she held Julia's gaze. It was secretive and intimate — definitely a sexy kind of smile, and Julia had to admit she liked it.

She wondered why she looked at Samantha this way. She always noticed attractive things about women and admired them, but not like this, where she was conscious of Samantha's sexual attractiveness. Maybe it was just that Samantha was the first lesbian she'd become really friendly with, and Samantha was awakening in her a greater awareness of female sensuality. The only thing wrong with that reasoning was that she'd known men all her life, and the truth was, she never even looked at men in quite the way she looked at Samantha.

A lot of men showed an interest in her but she'd only had four lovers in her whole life. If she was honest, it was because she didn't actually find men sexually attractive to look at. Other women did. The lovers she had chosen had approached her carefully and slowly, with a non-aggressive persistence. She realized, with a jolt, that her lovers had always taken the initiative sexually, and her pleasure came only from them touching her, the way she demanded to be touched. Her satisfaction, which was limited, only came from taking what she needed.

Her heart began to pound with anxiety. Why had it always been like this? Even with Ben, who she really cared about, who she knew loved her and always tried to make her feel good, sex was still, always, a one-dimensional experience.

She calmed herself by thinking that Samantha didn't turn her on either. She just noticed things about her, that was all, and she felt good with Samantha. God, she was thirty-three years old. If she had lesbian inclinations, surely she would have noticed long ago. You're obviously just not a very sexual person, she told herself.

She turned over and began to drift off to sleep, a persistent image lingering in the back of her mind, of Samantha's lips brushing against her own, Samantha's tiny gasp, and the surprising tingle she had felt in her body.

Samantha passed by Ruby's room and, seeing light coming from under the door, decided to drop in on her. Ruby answered wearing an oversized T-shirt. "Sam! How was dinner?"

Samantha flopped down on Ruby's bed. "Great. Too great. Julia's too gorgeous."

Ruby turned down the TV and looked at Samantha with a grin. "The drop-dead variety of gorgeous. Do you want a bourbon?" Samantha nodded and Ruby got them both a drink.

"I've got alarm bells ringing in my head like crazy, Ruby. I keep remembering the last time I fell for a straight woman."

Ruby handed Samantha her drink. "Oh, my God, you can't compare Julia with that silly woman." Ruby shook her head in disbelief. "She was just playing games, for Christ's sake." Ruby went over to the wardrobe and took a small container from one of her suitcases. She sat cross-legged on the bed beside Samantha and began to roll a joint. Samantha drained her glass at a gulp and lay on her back with her hands behind her head. "I could never work out what you saw in Elizabeth," Ruby said. "A married, Savannah, goddamn socialite, with 'straight as shit' engraved on her forehead." She lit the joint and took a couple of drags before handing it to Samantha. She chuckled. "Remember that party of hers you took me to?"

Samantha groaned. "Oh, don't remind me. That party really opened my eyes. That was when I began to realize I was her latest distraction — her little walk on the wild side." She took a deep drag on the joint. "I really don't know what came over me."

"Well, I seem to remember it was a particularly hot summer last year. I think you must've had heat-stroke, honey. Or maybe you were on the rebound from Mandy." Samantha looked at her in some confusion. "Well, after eighteen months, you thought you two had a future, and you took it pretty bad when she suddenly took off back to her ex in Virginia."

Bewildered, Samantha shook her head. "But that was a year before Elizabeth."

Ruby rolled her eyes. "I'm offering you excuses here, Sam, for your terrible judgment."

Samantha grinned and shrugged. "I'll take the heat-stroke."

"Fine. Anyway, I remember walking into that party and looking around at all those pretentious idiots and thinking, what's happened to Sam? That girl has gone mad!"

Samantha laughed and Ruby took another drag.

"They found you quite titillating, honey, being a famous dyke. I kept watching Elizabeth's husband trying to touch up the help, and wondered how he felt about his wife sleeping with Samantha Knight. He must've known — everyone else did." Ruby laughed and took another couple of drags. "They didn't find me quite so titillating though. They were all flashing their society smiles at me, but all the time they were looking down their well-bred noses and thinking, now why ain't that colored girl out in the kitchen?" They both broke up laughing.

"Remember that big-time lawyer who was hitting on you?"

Ruby's eyes shone in delight at the memory. "Yeah, I kept giving him the brush-off and walking away from him, but he wouldn't take the hint. He was the slimiest bastard I ever met. He followed me outside to the pool, walked up behind me and said real quiet, trying to be seductive, 'Would you like another glass of champagne, darling?' "

Samantha began rolling on the bed, hysterical. She loved this story.

"So, I said, 'Oh, is that what this is? And here's silly ol' me wondering how they got all these tiny bubbles into this cat's piss.' "

Samantha was shaking and wiping tears from her face.

Ruby looked at her with a serious expression. "Well, honey, for all Elizabeth's wealth, she served cheap champagne. You could pick her for new money a mile away." She took a long drag and passed the joint back to Samantha. "So, then the goddamn bastard smiles sweetly at me and puts his hand on my ass! So I just tossed my full glass of crap champagne all over his immaculate Armani crotch, and I said, 'Why, honey, ain't you ever been house-trained?' He just stood there blinking at me. Then I said, 'Ain't that your daughter over there? The one with the long blond hair and the pretty ass? She's much more my style, honey.' Then I hurled my empty glass into Elizabeth's pool and flounced off."

Samantha slowly recovered. Her stomach hurt from laughing. "The scary thing, Ruby, is I got taken right in. I thought it all meant something to Elizabeth. I'm worried I'm doing the same thing with Julia — seeing things that aren't really there."

Ruby lay down beside her, leaning on one elbow. Her eyes sparkled with interest. "Like what?"

Samantha stared up at the ceiling. "She looks at me in a certain way — it feels sexual. I'm so attracted to her, and it's hard to take. I'm sure she doesn't know the effect she's having on me, but if I didn't know better, I'd think she . . . you know . . . liked me too."

"What makes you so sure she doesn't? I only saw her for ten minutes and I estimate for nine of those ten minutes she was looking at you. Even when Lisa moved in on her, she was looking at you."

With a flush of irritation, Samantha remembered Lisa's pushing her out of the way. "Could you believe her, Ruby? She looked like she was about to eat Julia for dinner, for Christ's sake!"

Ruby grinned and said in a teasing tone, "And you were only saying this morning how well you thought Lisa was handling everything."

"Yeah, well . . . she's good at her job."

"You just don't wanna think about her handling Julia, do you?"

Samantha shook her head dismissively. "Julia's straight, Ruby."

Ruby laughed. "I checked her out and she ain't straight. She's got that vibe, honey, and I'll bet Lisa would say the same thing."

Samantha sighed impatiently. "She's got a goddamn boyfriend."

Ruby sat up and looked at Samantha in astonishment. "So? I had one of those things once, before I knew better! And I can tell you that screwing men is one very unpleasant habit that's extremely easy to give up." She smiled. "Julia just hasn't known the real thing yet. Now you've come into her life, and she's beginning to see the light."

Samantha looked away from Ruby, back at the ceiling. She didn't want to hear this.

"She's only known you for two days, honey, and

she mightn't know yet exactly what she's doing — looking you over that way — but I'll bet she's beginning to figure it out. That woman doesn't strike me as having a learning disability."

Samantha got up from the bed. "Well, I must admit, my dyke radar starting bleeping the moment I first looked at her." She headed for the door. "I've gotta go to bed. And we'd better hope our instincts are wrong, or I'm in big trouble."

"Why trouble, honey?"

Samantha hesitated for a moment, trying to make sense of her feelings. She ran her hand distractedly through her hair. "Julia's just . . . God, I don't know . . . just so different . . . special." Samantha closed her eyes for a second and groaned inwardly. "And she's the sexiest woman I've ever met in my goddamn life. We're only here for ten days, but I've got this feeling that if Julia showed me any encouragement, well . . . I'd fall for her in a big way. It sounds like a potential disaster situation, don't you think? Believing she's straight and out of bounds keeps it safe for me."

"It sounds like a love-at-first-sight situation to me." Ruby sighed. "You always make things so hard for yourself, Sam."

CHAPTER SIX

"Stand back, please," the security officer demanded. "Keep the walkway clear." His voice was raised above the screaming and yelling of Samantha's fans. About a thousand women were at Melbourne Airport to catch a glimpse of or maybe to touch Samantha as she was leaving for Sydney.

Samantha smiled and waved as she headed down the roped-off walkway leading to the VIP transit lounge. She greeted as many women as possible as she passed them, and endured many of them pulling at her clothes. A couple of them grabbed her and tried to kiss her, and she was glad to have Lisa at her side, leading her along as quickly as possible.

A microphone was shoved in front of her face by a pretty young reporter. "Could I ask you a few questions, Samantha?" She was blushing, looking very cute.

Samantha smiled at her. "I'm sorry I don't have time to stop, honey, but I wanna say I've had a great time in your beautiful city and I hope to come back real soon." There were blinding flashes all around her as photographers took her picture. She paused to sign a few autographs and a TV cameraman moved in on her.

"Just a couple of questions, Samantha," another reporter yelled.

Samantha smiled and waved and was glad to see the transit lounge door in front of her. Lisa opened it and quickly guided her inside. She had got the others through first, and they were sitting around drinking coffee. Samantha sat down with relief beside Ruby.

"I hope they're just as enthusiastic in Sydney," Ruby said.

"Yeah," Samantha answered vaguely, wondering where Julia was. "Did you see Julia out there, by any chance? We're leaving in fifteen minutes, I hope she doesn't miss the flight."

Ruby chuckled. "Can't you think about anything else but Julia?"

Samantha was about to justify herself, when the crowd outside suddenly erupted again with cheers and whistles.

Samantha went to the door and looked out the small window to see Julia coming up the walkway. A woman beside her was carrying a camera and camera cases — a baby-dyke who couldn't have been more than about twenty. They were obviously part of Samantha's party and that was enough to set the crowd off again.

Julia looked gorgeous in tight moleskin pants, an open-necked light-blue shirt and a long, open, silky-looking black vest. Her hands were in the pockets of her classic trench coat, and she walked with poise and elegance, apparently oblivious to the screams and yells from the women crowded on either side of her. Like a model on a catwalk, Samantha thought. She opened the door for them and they slid inside quickly.

Julia tossed her hair and sighed. "God, that walk felt like miles — it's good to be out of the crowd."

Julia suddenly looked a little flustered, and Samantha put her arm around her shoulders. "It's okay. You didn't look nervous out there. You looked like you were born for it."

Julia smiled. "You're used to it but I felt really exposed."

Samantha looked into her eyes and resisted a sudden urge to kiss her — her mouth was tantalizingly close. She could feel the warmth of Julia's body, and she took her arm away. She noticed the young woman who came in with Julia putting her camera gear down. "So this is our photographer?"

"Yes. This is Kerry Oliver." Kerry stood gazing at Samantha and a blush slowly spread from her neck to her face.

Samantha smiled and took Kerry's hand. "It's great to have you with us, honey." She kissed Kerry's cheek. "Come, I'll introduce you to everyone."

* * * * *

56

The flight to Sydney took around an hour and they were met at the airport by a similar-sized crowd of fans, who seemed to Julia to be particularly boisterous.

Lisa, with a few assistants from B.G.I., whisked them all out quickly through a rear exit into waiting limousines, and soon they were delivered to their hotel in the inner suburb of Elizabeth Bay, overlooking the harbor.

At reception, Julia ordered a copy of *The Sydney Morning Herald* to be delivered to her each morning. There would be some kind of feature about Samantha tomorrow in the lead up to her opening night, and she was looking forward to seeing it.

She settled herself into her room, hung up her clothes, put her cosmetics in the bathroom, then sat down at the table near the window and turned on her laptop. It was one-thirty, and she thought she'd order some lunch on room-service and make a start on her work, when the phone rang.

"I hope you're not working in there." Samantha's velvety voice had a teasing tone. "Lisa, Danny and I are having lunch in the dining room. Why don't you come and join us."

"Well, I was planning to get some work done this afternoon."

"But we only just got here. Come and have lunch, then come with us to the Opera House. We're gonna make sure all our stuff's arrived, and I wanna do a lighting check for tomorrow."

Julia smiled. "Okay, I'll see you in a few minutes. Why do I always find you so persuasive?" She heard Samantha's low, throaty chuckle.

"Well, honey, I really wouldn't know."

It was quite warm, so Julia took off her vest and shirt and put on a red, sleeveless top — leaving on her moleskins. She touched up her lipstick, grabbed a light jacket and went downstairs.

The dining room was crowded and Samantha kept an eye on the door, waiting expectantly for Julia. When she appeared, looking around, Samantha waved at her from the other side of the room. Julia's face lit up with one of her smiles, and she made her way over. Samantha couldn't take her eyes off her, and she noticed that Julia attracted the attention of almost everyone in the room as she moved between the tables.

Uncharacteristically, Danny stood up to greet her, and much to Samantha's annoyance, Lisa also stood, pulling out the chair beside her for Julia. They ordered a simple lunch of club sandwiches and light beer.

"I must congratulate you, Lisa, on the way you had everything organized at the airport earlier. It was handled with military precision," Julia said.

Lisa looked pleased and leaned close to Julia. "Well, I don't like to leave anything to chance. It's good to have the fans there — good for publicity — adds to the excitement of the concerts coming up and all that, but I like to get my people out quickly. I have a team of runners to pick up the gear, deliver it, and provide transport. The more smoothly these things happen, the happier the band is and the happier I am."

"The crowd here seemed to be a lot more pushy and noisy than in Melbourne."

Lisa smiled at Julia. It looked to Samantha like a suggestive little smile. "Well, you know Sydney. This is my hometown and we Sydney women don't hold back."

Samantha rolled her eyes.

Julia and Lisa knew a few people in common and they kept Samantha and Danny amused with their anecdotes about memorable past performers they'd met and tours they'd covered. Samantha knew she was being silly, but as the lunch progressed she found herself increasingly irritated by Lisa's monopoly of Julia's attention — especially when Lisa frequently touched Julia's arm or hand.

Julia looked across the table at Samantha, often, and gave special, private smiles, or so they seemed, and each time, Samantha experienced a delicious little tremor.

When they finished lunch, Julia called Kerry to bring her camera gear and join them, and at around three o'clock they left for the Opera House.

"Those blue and gold spotlights have to come on slowly . . . you know, a slow fade up as I start this song, okay?" Samantha was calling out instructions to the lighting director. While she was checking that he was following all the right cues from his running sheet for each song, Lisa and Danny were busy with some of the venue's staff, wandering on and off the stage, checking that the equipment and instruments were there and in working order.

Julia was sitting in one of the best seats in the house and Kerry was wandering around with her camera, changing lenses and experimenting with framing. Apart from a few staff members, they were the only ones watching the proceedings. Julia was preoccupied with Samantha.

Even without the excitement of an audience to create atmosphere, or her stage clothes and makeup, or the great sound of the band around her, Samantha had a powerful star quality. There was an aura about her as she moved around the stage, concentrating on her work. She strolled around with such confidence, she could have been in her own living room.

It seemed the lighting director wasn't getting it right, and Julia could perceive slight changes in Samantha. Her languid walk was becoming more brisk as she paced up and down the length of the stage, and there was a slight terseness in her voice.

"Okay," Samantha called, "I know the cues for this one are a bit complicated. You follow the sheet and I'll sing it for you."

The house lights went out, and gold and blue highlights shimmered magically on Samantha's hair and face. She was dressed simply in faded jeans and a black T-shirt, standing all alone on center stage, and Julia thought she looked utterly beautiful.

Samantha began to sing a gentle ballad and her voice was rich, pure and charged with emotion. There was a heart-wrenching poignancy to the impromptu performance, and Julia felt her throat tighten.

As the song went on, the backdrop changed from black to deep purple, then slowly to red. A number of white spotlights converged from different directions, capturing Samantha in a pool of light and the overall effect was enchanting. Julia felt every nerve in her body tingle and she was breathing quickly. She felt as if she had just woken up, with a jolt, from a dream. She realized she had been wandering happily, but ignorantly, over unfamiliar territory with Samantha in the last few days, observing and feeling things about her that she couldn't or wouldn't recognize.

The song was coming to an end and she felt herself turn a corner. There was no denying it — she was attracted to Samantha. She suddenly imagined holding her in her arms and kissing her beautiful mouth, those peach lips, and she felt an overwhelming wave of desire. She'd never felt like this, not ever.

Her eyes began to fill with tears, and she was starting to hyperventilate. She wanted to go outside, quickly, into the fresh air, outside to a world she recognized, of people jostling along the footpath, cars speeding down the street, boats bobbing in the harbor — ordinary things that she understood.

The song ended, and, except for the whirring and clicking of Kerry's camera, there was silence. Everyone seemed transfixed for a moment, then they burst into applause.

"That was great!" Samantha yelled to the lighting guy. She was smiling in satisfaction. The house lights came back on and Samantha looked up at Julia. "How did that look to you, Julia?"

Julia was trying to recover her composure. She swallowed. "It was perfect."

"Hey, everyone, did you hear that? That's good enough for me! I'm outta here. Let's go find a cold drink somewhere."

* * * * *

Lisa went home for the night and Danny returned to the hotel. Julia, Samantha and Kerry found a table at an outdoor restaurant beside the Opera House, overlooking the harbor where the boats and yachts were moored. It was six-thirty and the nearby bars and cafés were filling quickly with people who had finished work for the day. They ordered drinks and Kerry headed off to find the ladies' room.

It had been a warm, sunny day but a cool breeze had just sprung up off the water and Samantha slipped on the cotton jacket she'd brought with her. She was excited. Seeing the venue had settled her nerves. They'd have a rehearsal tomorrow afternoon, and she felt confident the shows here were going to be great.

She sipped her bourbon and looked at Julia. Her eyes were like sapphires in this twilight. Julia seemed quiet as she sat drinking her wine, watching the boats coming in. Suddenly Julia turned and looked at her in a way that made her hold her breath. There was something different in Julia's expression. Perhaps it was her imagination — those sexy eyes could be confusing — but there seemed to be something more overtly erotic about Julia. She glanced at Julia's mouth, then back at her eyes, half-consciously testing her. She didn't want to believe it, but Julia's expression became even more intimate. Samantha felt a sudden rush of desire, and she had to look away. She stared at the water, shimmering in the last light of the setting sun.

Kerry plopped down in the chair beside Samantha. "I got some really cool shots in there — portrait shots on the long lens. Fair dinkum, I reckon we're talking major poster material!"

Samantha liked Kerry's down to earth manner and bright enthusiasm. She imagined they'd get on well for the rest of the tour. She smiled. "Great! If you're fair dinkum, they must be good. Are either of you getting hungry? I'm starving."

"I have to get back to the hotel," said Kerry. "Ruby and I are going to a women's lounge bar tonight. Lisa told us about it. I don't know when she wants to leave."

"You're not letting that woman lead you astray now, are you, honey?"

Kerry rolled her eyes and sighed. "Oh, yeah, in my dreams."

"Well, you've both gotta eat first. I'll call Ruby and tell her to come over and join us. You can leave for the bar after dinner." Samantha took her cell phone from her jacket pocket and dialed the hotel.

"Maybe we can all go to the bar later."

"It's a lesbian bar, Julia," said Kerry. She sounded a little surprised that Julia would want to go there.

"I know that," said Julia in a casual tone.

Kerry shrugged indifferently, and twirled her glass around on the table, gazing at the harbor. Samantha's pulse quickened. Ordinarily, she'd think nothing of it, but she sensed a significance in Julia's interest in going to a dyke bar. There was a change in her.

Ruby answered the phone and she was preoccupied for a few minutes explaining to Ruby where they were.

She put her phone away. Julia was staring down at the table, slowly stroking the condensation from her glass. Samantha guessed it mightn't just be a fun night out that Julia had in mind, but a curiosity that was part of some sort of sexual awakening, which in all honesty, would be no great surprise. Samantha's heart began to pound. She felt caught between excitement and terror. If that was happening, she didn't want to be there and become a part of it. She couldn't get involved with Julia. It might be wiser to suggest to her that they go to a movie, or something.

Julia suddenly looked up at her with that same intensity in her eyes. She tossed her hair, and Samantha melted. She smiled. "Sure, we'll all go. It'll be fun."

They ordered another round of drinks and talked about other things, watching darkness settle over the harbor while they waited for Ruby, who arrived about a half-hour later.

"Why, there they are, honey!" They turned at the sound of Ruby's voice, which drowned out most other conversation in the restaurant. She gave the overwhelmed waiter a friendly pat on the arm and headed toward them. General conversation quieted and every patron stopped to watch Ruby as she swept majestically between the tables with a harmonious jangle of jewelry, clouds of delicious perfume and a riot of color. She kissed each of them on the mouth in greeting, attracting further stares from the other patrons.

"Why don't you let me order," suggested Julia. "I've been to this place lots of times. We can get a selection of dishes to share, and they have an incredible seafood pasta dish that's to die for." The others agreed that sounded great and soon they were enjoying their dinner.

"By the way, Ruby, we're all going to the lounge bar tonight," Samantha said. Ruby glanced at her with a subtle "I told you so" smile, then leaned over and kissed Julia's cheek.

"That's just great, Julia, honey! You're gonna love it. It sounds like a great place."

CHAPTER SEVEN

The lounge bar was in an imposing hotel built in the 1930s. Hoping to draw less attention to Samantha and Ruby, they arranged to enter in pairs. Julia and Samantha went in first, after buying their tickets in the foyer.

All around the softly lit room were small tables with pink tablecloths and candles glowing in glass holders. On a stage at one end, an all-women band was playing the sultry Latin rhythms of Sergio Mendes and Brazil 66.

Samantha spotted a vacant table for four and

guided Julia toward it. The pressure of Samantha's hand in the small of her back felt good and she was sorry when she took her hand away. Ruby and Kerry came in a few minutes later, and they waved them over.

A woman dressed in tiny black shorts and a matching cropped top came and took their drink order. The band was playing "Mas Que Nada" and the dance floor was filled with women dancing, holding one another close.

Some women, Julia noted, were dressed in dinner suits and others in cocktail dresses. She was relieved to see that many were also dressed casually in jeans and shirts, but regretted not changing into something special for this wonderful place.

She relaxed back in her chair and sipped her Campari and soda. At the next table, a woman dressed in a dinner suit replete with bow tie was smiling provocatively at her. She had cropped dark hair and red lipstick, and was smoking a cigar. Julia thought she was attractive and returned the smile. The woman slowly, suggestively, gave her the once-over. Julia kept smiling, surprised at how much she was enjoying the attention. Whenever men looked at her that way, she averted her eyes to discourage them.

Two women at another table were kissing passionately and she found the sight erotic. She imagined again kissing Samantha, and experienced a warm glow of desire. She closed her eyes for a moment, and when she opened them, the bow-tied woman was still gazing at her — still smiling.

Samantha, sitting beside her, was clearly amused. "I think she likes you." Her velvety voice felt like a caress.

Not as much as I like you.

A woman with a tray of cigars for sale came to their table.

"Ooh, yes, honey, I'll take one of those!"

"Yeah, cool! Me too!"

Ruby and Kerry lit their cigars and puffed away happily in a cloud of aromatic smoke. The woman at the next table was still looking at her. Julia smiled again and was filled with a delicious sense of happiness. All of this felt so right, and somehow comfortably familiar, although she'd never been in a situation like this before. She heard Samantha's sexy chuckle and turned to her.

"I think I'd better ask you to dance, honey, before she does."

Samantha held her hand as they walked onto the dance floor. The band had just begun to play the slow, Fifties, smoky jazz of Serge Gainsbourg. Samantha looked at Julia for a moment, then drew her into her arms and they began to dance.

Samantha's arms around her felt wonderful — the taut muscles of Samantha's back rippled under her hands and Samantha's breasts pressed against her own. She rested her cheek against Samantha's and breathed in her spicy fragrance. She could feel Samantha breathing faster, and she thought she heard Samantha murmur, "Oh, God." The warm glow of desire that had been rising and falling in gentle waves grew stronger, and Julia began to tremble.

She placed her arms around Samantha's shoulders, and Samantha wrapped her arms around her waist. They held each other close. Men's bodies felt nothing like this — never made her feel anything like this. Samantha's body was sleek and strong but womanly, soft and pliant, and the skin of her arms and face felt silky.

Julia imagined sliding her hands under Samantha's T-shirt and stroking her back. She felt a sudden rush of desire that made her ache. She slipped her thigh between Samantha's and they fitted together like one body. Samantha's hands moved slowly down, stroking her hips, and then she kissed Julia's neck. Julia gasped. The kiss burned into her and a fire ignited in her thighs.

Samantha's eyes were dark and her expression was of pure lust. She could feel Samantha trembling, and her own tremors increased. Their mouths were close, their lips almost touching. *Kiss me.*

"Excuse me!" A strange voice slowly penetrated Julia's brain. "Aren't you Samantha Knight?" Someone was tugging at Samantha's arm. The exquisite, sensual and private world Julia had possessed with Samantha suddenly evaporated.

Samantha appeared disoriented and turned to the group of women as if she was in a daze. Julia withdrew from her arms. Samantha looked at her with an expression of regret and squeezed her hand.

"I'll just go back to the table."

A dozen women moved in and Samantha was quickly surrounded.

Julia first went to the ladies room. She needed a moment to compose herself. She splashed cold water on her face and looked into the mirror. She felt so different, so changed, that she was almost surprised to see that she looked the same. She ran her hands through her hair, then applied some lipstick that she had in her pocket. She took a deep breath and returned to the table.

"Sam's been spotted has she, honey? It was inevitable." Ruby was still puffing away on her cigar and Kerry was draining her glass of beer.

Julia was still nursing an erotic, dull ache and didn't feel quite herself. She nodded at Ruby.

"I got you another Campari." She looked at Ruby beside her and suddenly, inexplicably, felt like bursting into tears. Ruby smiled gently and kissed her cheek. "It's okay, honey," she whispered.

Kerry was staring at her, wide-eyed. She'd obviously seen the sensual way she and Samantha had been dancing, and probably thought it was odd behavior for her supposedly straight boss, Julia thought. She didn't care. From the corner of her eye, she saw Ruby give Kerry a little shove.

A few minutes later, Samantha returned and sat beside Julia. Under the table she squeezed Julia's hand, then released it. She gave Julia a perfunctory smile; their special moment had passed and Samantha was her usual self again.

It wasn't long before another group of fans approached looking for autographs, so they quickly finished their drinks.

Back at the hotel, on the way to the lifts, Samantha paused outside the hotel bar. "Would you have a coffee with me, Julia?"

They said goodnight to the others and found a table inside the intimate, cozy bar. It was for hotel guests only, and there were few other people there. Nondescript music was playing unobtrusively and the lamplight was low.

They ordered coffee and sat silently. Samantha looked into her eyes for a long moment and Julia sensed her perplexity. Then Samantha looked down at the table and fiddled with a cocktail menu. Her golden hair glinted in the lamplight and shadows played on her beautiful face. She was biting her lower lip and Julia longed to kiss her. Looking at Samantha's hands, she wished she could feel them on her again.

The waiter placed their coffee on the table. Julia was at a loss to express herself. Her desire for Samantha was so great that she couldn't think clearly — she felt completely out of her depth. She wanted Samantha to take control of the situation. "I'm not sure exactly what's happening to me."

Samantha spooned sugar into her coffee and stirred it. "It's okay, these things happen. It's my fault. I'm terribly attracted to you and have been since I first met you."

Julia didn't want her to back off. She wanted Samantha to at least help her to understand her feelings. She'd know what to do. "Samantha, I wanted you tonight like I've never wanted anyone in my life." Samantha put her hand over her forehead, as if shielding her eyes. "And I still want you now." Samantha seemed to shudder slightly and Julia saw her swallow hard.

"God, you don't hold anything back do you, honey."

Julia felt tears coming to her eyes. Everything was happening so fast. She glanced away, unseeing, around the room, concentrating on not crying.

Samantha placed a hand on hers and a powerful current ran up Julia's arm, coursing through her body. The tears spilled down her cheeks and Julia caught the glint of tears in Samantha's eyes, too.

"Baby . . ." The word was like a kiss, and Julia felt faint. "I could do what I'm aching to do, and take you upstairs to bed." Her voice was barely more than a whisper. Julia shuddered and Samantha's grip on her hand tightened. "But I know you're feeling confused, baby, and I know it's a big mistake getting to the bedroom feeling confused." Julia wiped at her tears. "Maybe this is an aberration for you, honey, but if not, and we start an affair, it's only gonna make things very difficult for us. I'm going home in ten days and there's no point starting something that's got nowhere to go." Samantha paused and blinked away her tears. "I think we should concentrate on just being great friends. I don't wanna lose that." She pushed her untouched coffee away. "I think we should call it a night, don't you? We've got a big day tomorrow — opening night."

"I'll just stay here on my own for a few minutes longer."

Samantha stood. She looked shaken — her eyes were still dark and passionate. "Goodnight, Julia." Then she left.

The next morning was Friday. It had taken Julia quite a while to get to sleep the night before and when she woke, her mind was filled again with Samantha. As she recalled the moment during the lighting check when she recognized her desire for Samantha, and as she remembered Samantha's arms around her, she felt a rush of lust. Her heart began to pound in trepidation.

In the bright, sunny reality of the morning after, those events seemed unreal. If it wasn't for the persistent ache in her body, she wouldn't believe it had all actually happened. The phone rang, and she jumped.

Ben was calling to tell her that he missed her, and that it looked like he could get a few days off to meet her somewhere in north Queensland when her job was finished. He was looking forward to it.

Julia was relieved to hear his voice, and the erotic images of Samantha quickly vanished from her mind. They chatted for a while about comforting, familiar things — day-to-day matters, the ordinary things that made up the organized life she had created for herself.

She had a shower, then her breakfast and newspaper arrived, and she sat down at the table. She turned on her computer and checked her e-mail. There was a message from the art director, wanting to discuss ideas with her about the feature layout. She'd contact him later. She sipped her coffee and tried to think about how good it would be to see Ben again. They hadn't spent any time together for so long and they'd have a lot to talk about. She leafed through the paper to see what had been written about Samantha's arrival in town and impending concert. There was a half-page story with a photo taken at the airport.

Suddenly, a vision of Samantha gazing into her eyes, crashed into her mind with a shocking jolt that took her breath away. She reached unsteadily for her coffee cup and knocked it over.

While she mopped up the mess, she tried to put her feelings into some kind of perspective. This was all a bit silly and had got out of hand, she thought. Of course she enjoyed the lounge bar last night. It was an all-women's venue — of course she felt at home there. That was no big deal, and what happened with Samantha was an aberration — just as Samantha said.

She had gotten carried away, that was all. Thank goodness Samantha had the sense to know that.

Then she pictured Samantha's face — her eyes glinting with tears as she whispered, "Baby . . ." Julia sank into a chair as another weakening tremor overtook her. Her hands shook as she poured herself another cup of coffee.

She should be pleased that Samantha had somehow awakened in her sexual responses that she hadn't known she was capable of. Obviously a deep passion had been lying dormant within her, and perhaps she could now expect more from her relationships. Maybe it *was* time to move on from Ben — he could never make her feel this way. She just hadn't met the right person yet — just as Samantha said.

She had to put these thoughts out of her mind and concentrate on the work she had planned for the day. She had arranged to meet Louis, Jenny and Don by the pool at nine before they left for their rehearsal, and she was meeting Danny later for lunch to get all their background stories. That evening she was going to the concert and she looked forward to gauging the response from the first Sydney audience.

She had time for a swim before the others arrived to meet her at the pool. She put on her bathing suit and terrycloth robe, grabbed a towel, her notes and tape recorder and headed down to the secluded garden.

Later that day, Julia was sitting at the table in her room making notes from the conversations she'd recorded earlier — putting them into a logical order.

She smiled as she listened to Danny's voice on the tape. It had been an enjoyable lunch. She learned that his career in the music business had begun over twenty years ago when he was a guitarist in a moderately successful band. In his own words, he lacked the talent to ever be really great, and he moved into the management side of the business. At first, Samantha was only one of the performers he managed, but he soon dropped his other clients as her popularity escalated. There was no doubting the enormous thrill he got from being a part of Samantha's fame and success. His eyes shone, and he squirmed excitedly in his seat as he described memorable concerts and nerve-racking contract negotiations. He provided some fascinating insights to the music business generally, and had been very entertaining.

She paused and leaned back in her chair, sipping her mineral water as she read through a fax Adele had sent her. It included copies of reviews Samantha had received during her U.S. tour, and they'd be useful for her story. She checked her watch. It was five-thirty. She should finish up for the day, she thought, and get ready for the concert. She was meeting Kerry in the hotel bistro for dinner at seven, before they headed off together to the Opera House. She tidied up her notes, then went to the bathroom and had a shower.

As she applied her makeup, she was aware of a growing tension. She'd had a lot to think about during the day, spending much of her time in the company of other people, and she'd been able to push her worrying feelings about Samantha to the back of her mind. But thought of seeing her on stage, later, made her tingle with anticipation and anxiety.

She dressed in fitted black pants and a fitted cream-colored satin jacket. She slipped on a fine gold chain, added simple gold earrings and sprayed on her perfume. Suddenly, she remembered Samantha's arms around her — her hands moving down to her hips, and she trembled. She took a deep breath, then applied a deep rose-pink lipstick. Stop being ridiculous, she chided herself. Behave like a professional.

She grabbed her purse and headed downstairs to meet Kerry.

The audience was screaming and applauding. The auditorium of the Opera House was packed, the atmosphere electric. Samantha strode out onto the stage and stood in the spotlight.

"All right," she growled deep and low, and the audience screamed louder.

She was wearing a white suit with tails. There was no shirt under the jacket, which was cut to reveal a glimpse of her cleavage. She had a glittering, hot pink bow tie around her throat. From her press seat close to the stage, Julia could see her clearly. Her tanned skin was glowing and her mouth was a glossy pink. Sexy, Julia thought, her mind shimmering once again with erotic memories of last night. She closed her eyes in an attempt to quell the desire that rippled through her. Couldn't she control these feelings, for God's sake?

She looked at the enraptured faces around her and wondered how many of these other women felt as she did. How many of them fantasized about Samantha too? How many times, in how many cities, had Samantha held a woman the way she held her last night? Perhaps it was just her own ego that made her think Samantha's attraction for her was special, or perhaps it was her lack of experience with real desire.

She turned her attention back to the stage. She had to be objective about the performance, and stop indulging herself. The staging was excellent, and Samantha and the others were in fine form. She wondered, again, at Samantha's voice. If life had taken a different turn for her she could quite feasibly be performing opera in this famous auditorium. She would've made a great mezzo.

The lighting and the pace of the music changed, and suddenly, Samantha was bathed in highlights of blue and gold. Julia's skin prickled. Samantha began to sing the ballad that had affected Julia so powerfully the day before. Julia bit her lip and forced herself to hold back her tears. At the end of the first verse, Samantha gave her a quick glance, and Julia trembled as a wave of desire washed over her. God! It was no use just trying to push these feelings out of her mind. Her sexual response to just the sight of Samantha was preventing her from thinking clearly. The best thing to do, she decided, was keep away from her for a couple of days — at least over the weekend. They were flying to Brisbane on Tuesday, and, hopefully, in the meantime she could get all this into some perspective.

Before the concert was over, she slipped out quietly and returned to the hotel.

* * * * *

On Saturday morning, Julia sat at the table near the open window in her room, with her breakfast of coffee and toast. The sky was a perfect blue with a few high, cotton-ball clouds, and the warmth in the gentle breeze promised a hot day. Just like yesterday, she'd woken up with Samantha on her mind. She trembled at every thought of her, and knew her attraction to Samantha was growing like a hunger. Was this the passion and desire that everyone talked about, that she'd always craved? It was difficult to deal with the fact that it had taken a woman to bring this out in her. Why hadn't she ever felt this way about a woman before?

She had thought her self-knowledge was pretty good. Afterall, she had relationships all figured out. It had taken her ten years to get to know herself and carve out a comfortable and successful niche for herself. Years ago, she had ceased to be concerned that she didn't fall madly in love the way her friends did. She'd practiced the conversations, had all the explanations and excuses, and handled with aplomb the regular inquiries from her parents and friends about when she was going to settle down, get married and have a family. These things didn't bother her anymore. She felt at ease with herself, if not entirely happy. It seemed unbelievable that it had taken Samantha Knight just five days to turn her cozy world upside down.

She sighed, and pushed her plate away. She'd better try and get some work done. She picked up the paper and turned to the review of Samantha's opening night. She rolled her eyes at the headline: "What a Knight! Samantha Rocks The Opera House." It was an excellent review as she expected.

She turned on her laptop. Mechanically, with her mind only half on the job, she set up the format and headers to begin writing her article, then she gazed out of the window again at the harbor.

Her closest emotional relationships, she knew, were with her female friends, and she was well aware they meant more to her than to them. Even then, something prevented her from sharing all her feelings with them. But she felt completely different with Ruby, Lisa, even Kerry, and Samantha — especially Samantha. With them, she felt totally at home. She remembered Thursday night at the lounge bar and how the bow-tied woman had flirted with her. Julia had flirted back, and loved it.

She focused on the computer screen and began to type:

The lights change and Samantha stands completely still looking at us. There's a tension in her that we can all feel and we're tense too. The pulsing rhythm of the bass guitar is slow, and arouses a primitive, mysterious anxiety in us. Samantha's misted with sweat and her eyes are focused on one woman — every woman — on me, and there's a desperation and a passion in her that's compelling and frighteningly alluring.

The acoustic guitar comes in with slowly building chords, and the beat picks up — in time with our hearts. Samantha's lips are almost touching the microphone, and then she takes a breath — her breathing, in and out, is deliberately sexy and we hold our breath . . . waiting.

Her voice is sultry as she begins to sing. She's holding back, but we know that soon, she's going to explode. "I've been watching you, baby,/ I've been catching your smiles,/ You're holding her hand/ But I know all the while . . .".

We're all caught by the accusation in her voice and we know that Samantha can see inside us — she knows what we're thinking. She takes another slow breath that makes us shudder.

She wouldn't go to the concert tonight, she decided. If she was home, she might spend the evening at a friend's house. Maybe Jane and Robert would be holding one of their wonderful dinner parties. Helena and Don, Vicki and Adrian, and Justine — currently single — would be there. The conversation would be controversial and witty. Julia would be with Ben. He would look at her frequently and often take her hand and gently kiss it while he gazed into her eyes. He would expect to spend the night with her and she would think: it's been a while — why not? And they'd go home together and have sex, and it would be OK, and the next morning, after coffee in the garden, she would start to wish he would leave.

"You can feel the wind of change,/ You wanna take a chance,/ I know you wanna touch the fire/ You wanna learn my dance . . ."

Samantha's voice is loud now, and powerful. She's striding around the stage, agitated, urgently longing for something or someone frustratingly out of her reach — and I know she's talking to me. I want to know her like I've never known anyone — I want to be her and for her to be me.

And if her voice resonates wildly inside my body

and her words cut into me, her every orgasmic breath
totally thrills me.

The phone rang. It was Kerry asking if Julia wanted to join them all for lunch. Interesting that Samantha didn't call to ask, she thought. "Thanks, Kerry, but I think I'll spend this weekend getting a good start on the story. I won't go to the concert tonight, but you don't need me there — you'll be fine."

As she hung up the phone, Julia wondered if Samantha was thinking about her. Was Samantha feeling the same desire for her? Was that why she hadn't contacted her yesterday or today? Of course, she had other things to think about, but perhaps she was annoyed with her. Perhaps she thought Julia was just a tease — playing games. God, the thought was horrifying. She couldn't bear for Samantha to think that way about her.

Julia put aside her work. She suddenly felt tired and uninspired, and in the heat of the afternoon, she lay down on the bed. She pictured herself at home, sitting up in her own comfortable bed with loads of pillows around her, reading a book. She had a cup of coffee on the bedside table and Magpie was curled up asleep beside her. The sun was spilling in through the full-length windows, and half the leaves on the oak tree in her front garden had already fallen. Through the branches, she could make out the park across the road. The comforting image lulled her to sleep for the rest of the afternoon.

That evening, she ordered dinner on room service, and relieved about her decision to stay away from the concert, settled down and watched a movie.

On Sunday, Julia took out the notes she had made
on Friday about Danny and the others and tried to
focus her mind on the story. But her thoughts kept
wandering. She felt her familiar self-image drifting
away, and the more she tried to hold onto it, the more
nebulous it became. Not seeing Samantha or speaking
with her hadn't subdued Julia's desire at all, and she
missed Samantha's company.

Late in the morning, she sat down at her
computer. She opened the document she began writing
yesterday, and read it. "For God's sake, wake up!" she
muttered. *What do you think a lesbian is?* She had
changed since she met Samantha. She sighed. She'd
changed into herself. She couldn't imagine how she
would reconcile this with the lifestyle she had
established, but she couldn't think that far ahead. The
only thing she was certain about was her desire for
Samantha, and having accepted that, she knew she
had to follow her heart.

Samantha's reticence was understandable. The fact
of her leaving in a week's time frightened her, but if
Samantha felt the same way she did, they would find
a solution. Her major concern now was how Samantha
felt.

Julia decided to stay away from the concert again.
She would contact Samantha tomorrow and arrange to
meet with her. Hopefully, it would make an important
difference to Samantha to know that Julia had
thought things over and come to these conclusions.
Samantha would know then that she was no longer
confused, and was serious about pursuing a
relationship.

Julia marked the text on the screen then hit the delete key. She should concentrate on her work and start writing something she could let other people read. There was one important thing she had to do before meeting Samantha, though, and it filled her with dread. She had to phone Ben, and tell him their affair was over.

CHAPTER EIGHT

By late Monday morning, Julia had written a rough draft of her story. There were still many details to be added, and she needed to talk more with Samantha to complete the picture. She was glad about that. Even if Samantha was annoyed with her, this would give them a reason to get together.

Adele had phoned earlier to see how things were going, and asked to see the draft and photos to date so she could plan the space in the magazine. The shots Kerry had taken at the Opera House during Thursday's lighting check had been processed, and

Julia thought they were outstanding. She sent the file by modem to Adele, then called Kerry to send the negatives by overnight courier. Wanting some fresh air and exercise after being cooped up in her room for the last couple of days, she decided to go for a swim. She'd call Samantha when she got back. Today was a rest day for the band and she wanted to ask Samantha to have dinner with her.

When she came back into her room a half-hour later, her phone was ringing. She quivered at the sound of Samantha's sexy voice. "I think you've been working way too hard in there, honey, and it's time you came out to play."

A rush of desire swept through her and stopped at her throat, making it difficult to talk. She swallowed. "I was thinking the same thing. I was just going to call you."

Samantha chuckled — that low, throaty chuckle that she liked so much. "Well, now, I'm sure glad to hear that. Ruby, Lisa and I are going to take a walk over to King's Cross and find a café for lunch. Why don't you join us?"

Julia's spirits rose. Samantha wasn't annoyed with her, at least. "Sounds good. I'll meet you downstairs in twenty minutes."

It was warm outside, so she put on an aqua camisole and tucked it into her jeans, dried her hair, and applied a little makeup. She added a spray of perfume, then headed downstairs.

Samantha was waiting in the lobby not far from the elevator bank with Lisa and Ruby. She turned when she heard the doors open and felt a tremor of lust when she saw Julia. She was wearing those great-fitting faded jeans and a top that showed every inch of her gorgeous figure. She tossed her hair and dropped one of her breathtaking smiles. As Julia kissed her cheek, engulfing Samantha's senses with her seductive fragrance, Samantha was greatly relieved to see that Julia was as warm toward her as ever.

She had been worried that Julia might regret what took place between them and be angry at her. Julia had obviously been avoiding her, and although she'd been tempted to phone her many times over the weekend, she'd decided to let her take her own time.

Samantha smiled and touched Julia's hand. "I sure have missed you, honey — we all have."

"Yeah, girl, what've you been writing in there? *War and Peace*?" Ruby gave her a hug, and they all set off into the sunshine.

Almost immediately, Lisa draped her arm around Julia's shoulders and somehow managed to steer her in front of Samantha and Ruby. "So, how's the feature coming along?" Lisa asked.

Samantha felt a flush of irritation. Lisa could be so damned pushy. "Lisa? How does Angela feel about your coming with us to Brisbane tomorrow?" Angela was Lisa's girlfriend. "Does she miss you when you're away?" Samantha hoped her tone didn't reveal her annoyance.

Lisa turned to her. "As you well know, we have a very relaxed, open relationship. She's got her own life to lead. We don't believe in monogamy — *we're* not possessive." Her tone was cutting.

Samantha smirked as Lisa removed her arm from Julia's shoulder.

Ruby gave her a nudge and grinned. "That shot missed the mark, honey. And I can't help noticing your eyes are definitely looking greener today — it must be the light."

They wandered around the Cross, past sleazy bars, strip joints, a few fashionable boutiques and restaurants. The sex workers paraded up and down the street. Every city seemed to have a similar place, Samantha thought. It was like walking around in a bad movie. They chose a café and sat at a table in the sun. They ordered baguettes and cappuccinos, and watched the tourists and streetwalkers pass by as they ate their lunch.

Ruby flicked back her long hair, her bracelets and bangles tinkling like wind-chimes. "You must be nearly finished with that article, Julia. Have you done the bit about me yet?" Her eyes sparkled.

Julia laughed. "There are lots of bits about you in different parts of the story, but I haven't finished yet." She turned to Lisa. "I'd like to talk to you about the promotion side of things at some stage."

Lisa looked pleased and Samantha thought the smile she gave Julia was practically lewd. "Yeah, great. We can get together in Brisbane. There's heaps of information and stories I can give you."

Samantha felt her hackles rise. *Yeah, and I know what else.*

"I need to talk more with you too, Samantha. I need your perspective on the background information I've gathered." Julia's gaze was direct and engaging, and for a moment, Samantha felt hypnotized. Her expression was almost conspiratorial, tinged with seductive promise. She gave her hair a little toss and Samantha felt the latent heat in her body flicker into a low flame.

She was glad Julia wasn't mad at her, but she'd hoped fervently that Julia's passion would have cooled off by now. She didn't know how she could resist her again. Samantha swallowed and smiled. "Yeah, of course."

"Well, you'd better do it soon," Ruby said, " 'cause we're leaving in just six days. Doesn't time fly?"

Samantha quickly glanced at Julia, who averted her eyes and began drawing patterns in the bread crumbs on the table. Julia seemed as stung by Ruby's reminder as she was.

"Do you have someone waiting for you at home, Samantha?" Lisa's tone was snide.

"Well, Donna and Candice live close by and keep an eye on the house when I'm away. And there's Tom and Mike, who live across town and tend to mother me. I'm looking forward to seeing them all again."

"I was thinking more about a lover waiting for you."

Julia visibly tensed. "No," Samantha said.

Lisa laughed dryly, without humor. "I find that a bit hard to believe. Women are throwing themselves at you all the time."

Samantha was beginning to feel angry. Lisa was obviously playing this game for Julia's benefit. Samantha knew she'd started it all and should let it drop, but couldn't. "Believe it or not, Lisa, I don't meet that many women I actually wanna sleep with. Not all of us fuck around at any opportunity."

Lisa's face colored slightly. No doubt she was about to come back with another smart remark when, thankfully, Ruby cut in. "Not like me. I'm just terrible, ain't I, Sam?" She fluttered her eyelashes, and Samantha was glad that Julia laughed. "I think we should be getting back. I want an early night — I'm beat," Ruby said.

They stood up to leave and Lisa suddenly said, "Julia, why don't we have dinner tonight and you can ask me those questions."

"Sorry, Lisa. Julia's already having dinner with me," Samantha snapped.

Julia gave Samantha one of her smiles and Samantha felt a dangerous tremor. God, how was she going to cope with that smile and those eyes all during dinner? But she had to see her — she missed her.

As Lisa walked on ahead with Julia again, Ruby hissed, "For God's sake, Sam, what's got into you? I've never seen you like this. You're behaving like a jealous schoolgirl!"

"Lisa just gets on my nerves. She won't leave her alone. She doesn't need Lisa coming onto her like that."

"Julia can look after herself. She doesn't look too bothered to me."

Samantha scowled. She knew she was being ridiculous, but Julia just made her crazy.

"Well, I think you and Lisa should get it all over with once and for all," Ruby went on. "Why don't you two go find some quiet, long, dusty street some place, and have a shoot-out at sundown, honey."

Samantha didn't find the idea very funny and she rolled her eyes. That only seemed to amuse Ruby more and she giggled, aggravatingly, all the way back to the hotel.

Lisa said goodbye to them at the hotel entrance. She was going back to her office at B.G.I. in the city. As Ruby headed for the elevators, Julia touched Samantha's arm. "I'll meet you here at eight o'clock, okay? I'll book somewhere. Is Thai all right?"

Samantha trembled at her touch and at the thought of being alone with her later. "Yeah, great, honey. That's fine."

Back in her room, Julia booked a table at a restaurant she liked on the other side of the harbor. It was a quiet and intimate place where she could talk to Samantha.

While she got ready, her mind was racing. Samantha wanted to spend time with her! She wondered why Samantha was jealous of Lisa's attention toward her. She wasn't sure whether the interest Lisa showed her was genuine or just playful. In any case, it didn't worry her, and there was no need for Samantha to be bothered by it.

She decided to go to dinner prepared to talk about the magazine article. If Samantha was going to play it cool, Julia didn't think she could cope with small talk.

She dressed in a lightweight red suit. The skirt was fitted and quite short, and the jacket, also fitted, was cropped at the waist with broad shoulders. It had a round neckline and buttoned to just below her throat.

Samantha had also had a couple of days to think things over, and perhaps she wouldn't allow any intimacy between them again. Julia desperately hoped otherwise.

She put on her small gold earrings and a red-tinted lip gloss. She hoped Samantha had been burning up like she was. She sprayed on her perfume. She wanted to make love with Samantha tonight. The thought made her quiver with desire, but it also made her nervous. It would be the final, irreversible step toward a new future, and she was acutely aware of her lack of experience. It appalled her to think she might disappoint Samantha. *What if I'm no good at it?*

With men, she had never cared about being a good lover. She knew, in fact, she wasn't, but had considered it to be their problem. Now she cared a lot. Every nerve in her body seemed to be pulsing with a new sensuality, and making Samantha happy really mattered.

As the waiter poured their wine, Julia gazed at Samantha across the table. She was wearing a loose-fitting linen suit — jacket and pants — in light gray with a fine maroon pinstripe. Her white shirt underneath was open at the neck and her sleeves were casually pushed up. A thin gold chain just met her cleavage.

Samantha gulped the remainder of her bourbon. "I think I'll go for another one of these before I start on the wine," she said to the waiter. She smiled at Julia. "You look beautiful tonight."

"Thank you. So do you," Julia said as Samantha's eyes grew darker. Julia felt a tremor, and saw Samantha swallow. It was an awkward moment.

Samantha glanced away and began biting on her lip. "I've brought some notes and my tape recorder. I thought I'd tell you what I've got about the others' backgrounds, and get your comments. Then we can talk about your songs and what inspires them."

Samantha smiled brightly, clearly relieved. "Yeah, great." The waiter brought Samantha's bourbon and she drank it in two gulps.

Their first course arrived: tiny spring rolls with a hot, sweet dipping sauce and a warm beef salad flavored with lime juice, coriander and chili. Julia turned on the tape recorder and they talked about Samantha's music and the band while they ate.

Animated by the subject, when Samantha talked about her songs, and arranging them musically with Ruby, her eyes sparkled and her face lit up with her gorgeous smile. She had to be the sexiest woman in the world, Julia thought. No wonder so many women adored her.

The food was good but Julia found the butterflies in her stomach had dampened her appetite. Samantha was picking at her food too. The main course of red curry with chicken and asparagus, and a dish of rice, arrived along with another bottle of wine and a third bourbon for Samantha.

Julia turned off the tape recorder. Samantha wasn't making it easy, but Julia had important things to tell her. "I want to tell you that I've broken up with Ben."

Samantha downed some bourbon. "Good. You weren't happy — you deserve better."

"There's more to it than that."

Samantha looked into her eyes for a long moment, then looked down and twirled her hair.

"I'm finished with men, Samantha. I've come to understand that they never suited me because I'm not made that way."

Samantha looked up, her expression serious. "What do you mean?"

Julia smiled. "What do you think I mean? Do I have to say the L-word? Is that the test of my sincerity?" Samantha didn't flinch but held Julia's gaze. "Okay, I'm a lesbian. Do I pass?"

Samantha swallowed the rest of her bourbon. "I'll just order another one of these." Her voice was husky.

"Do you really need another one, darling?" God! *Darling*. It just came out. Samantha looked shaken. Tears glinted suddenly in her eyes, and her gaze strayed to Julia's mouth, lingering, making Julia feel weak.

"No, I don't need another one." Samantha's voice was little more than a whisper.

"You must know that you've made a big impact on me — on my life. My feelings for you have made me think about things that have confused me for years. What happened the other night was no aberration. It's made everything fall into place."

Samantha swallowed and took a deep, ragged breath. "It's a big step you've taken, but of course, I'm not surprised. You might find some things difficult for a while, you know, but you'll be very happy, I'm sure of that." Her voice caught and she put her hand over her eyes for a moment, as if trying to control her emotions. "But, Julia, we did the right thing the other night. There's no point in us starting anything." She looked up. "You know that, don't you?"

Julia held her gaze. She wanted to say no, she didn't agree, but she didn't want to put any more pressure on Samantha. She looked upset enough. More tears welled in Samantha's eyes and Julia blinked away tears of her own. She didn't want to upset Samantha, and she couldn't, in the restaurant, take her in her arms and comfort her, although she desperately wanted to. She changed the subject. "We got some photo proofs back this morning — they're fabulous. Kerry's done a great job."

Samantha seemed to brighten a little, and for the rest of the meal, their conversation concerned the concerts and speculation about the audiences in Brisbane. Neither of them ate much of the main course either, but Samantha seemed more relaxed. Julia didn't know whether that was due to the alcohol, or whether she had come to terms with what Julia had told her, but by the end of the dinner, she had no doubt that Samantha still wanted her.

They left the restaurant and crossed the road to the taxi rank. "Maybe you'd like to see the shots. We could order coffee in my room."

Samantha hesitated for a moment, then gave Julia one of her sexy half-smiles. "Sure, honey, I'd like to see them." For a split-second, Julia thought she'd faint.

Back at the hotel, Julia flicked on a lamp and watched Samantha slip off her jacket and toss it over one end of the sofa. Julia loved Samantha's casual, languid gestures. She pictured Samantha striding over to her, taking Julia in her arms and kissing her passionately.

Samantha rolled up her shirt sleeves and stood with her hands in her pockets, looking at her, and Julia shivered as a wave of desire washed over her. Her eyes dark, Samantha began biting her lip, then she glanced away. "Maybe I'll take a bourbon and skip the coffee."

As Julia fixed her drink, she could feel Samantha's scrutiny. Her heart racing, Julia poured herself a brandy and set the glasses down on the coffee table. She sat on the sofa and indicated the folder on the table containing the proofs. "These are the shots I wanted to show you."

Samantha sat beside her, picked up her drink and gulped half of it. Julia leaned back on the sofa and sipped her brandy, watching her. She crossed her legs slowly, and saw Samantha glance at them. Samantha gulped down the rest of her drink, then took the proofs from the folder.

Julia moved closer to her and gently took them from her hand. "They're all good, but these are outstanding." She showed Samantha her favorite shots. Samantha stared at them without comment. Her mind appeared to be elsewhere. Julia breathed in her enchanting perfume and wondered, frantically, why Samantha wouldn't touch her. She knew Samantha wanted to. Samantha closed her eyes for a moment and took a deep breath. Julia couldn't take much more. She desperately wanted to be kissed. "Samantha," she murmured.

Suddenly, Samantha stood up and crossed the room, her back to Julia. "I'm sorry, I can't cope with this." Her voice was ragged. She grabbed her jacket and headed for the door. Julia got up and went to her. She reached out to touch her arm and Samantha stepped back. "Don't, honey," she whispered, as tears welled in her eyes.

"I want you stay with me tonight."

Samantha looked distressed as she shook her head.

"I'm going home on Sunday and I can't start an affair with you that'll be over in less than a week." She looked away with a helpless expression, biting her lip. "You mean too much to me for that." She shielded her eyes for a moment, composing herself. "Maybe it wouldn't bother you too much, but it would seriously bother me."

She opened the door and gave Julia a last, passionate glance. "I'm sorry, baby." Then she was gone.

Julia couldn't believe it. Samantha had been there, wanting her, and she let her go. She had stood gazing at Samantha, practically willing her into her arms, but didn't go to her. She could have so easily kissed Samantha when they were sitting close together on the sofa, but didn't. She had waited for Samantha to make all the moves.

Tears of frustration rolled down her cheeks as she realized she had spent her life expecting someone else to take the initiative. Samantha was allowing her fears about the future to overshadow their powerful attraction for each other, while Julia believed their feelings were all that mattered. They could deal with longer-term issues later. None of that was important now. Samantha, as intelligent as she was, obviously wasn't right about everything.

She got into bed, trying to ignore the ache that wouldn't go away. Giving up on Samantha wasn't an option — she wanted her too much for that, and she was obviously going to have to become more assertive than she had been. Next time would be different, she thought. She closed her eyes and imagined seducing Samantha — pictured her yielding in her arms — and her desire grew stronger.

She trailed her hand down her naked body. She was sweating. She touched herself, quivering as pleasure rippled through her. She was so wet. She thought about Samantha — holding her, kissing her. She gasped and shuddered and lay still, catching her breath, her heart pounding. Next time, she thought, she wouldn't let Samantha say no.

CHAPTER NINE

Julia left the hotel with Kerry earlier than the others on Tuesday morning. She wanted Kerry to get a series of shots showing Samantha making her way through the clamorous crowd of fans as she headed to the departure lounge for their flight to Brisbane. She and the art director had discussed the layout, and planned to place the shots vertically, as strips of film, down each page of her story. They'd get more shots in Brisbane too, especially on Sunday when Samantha left to fly home.

Julia felt panic grip her each time she thought of

Samantha's leaving. Eleven o'clock, Sunday morning. She couldn't imagine letting things stand as they were between them and simply saying goodbye, which was what Samantha apparently intended. She wondered how she would overcome Samantha's obstinacy and find an opportunity to talk with her, to be with her. Samantha was without doubt a headstrong woman, used to having things her own way.

When she and Kerry arrived, a crowd of several hundred women, some TV crews and security staff were already waiting for Samantha. Julia's mobile rang and she went inside the departure lounge to take the call. It was Adele, calling to say she loved the draft and photos.

Suddenly, screaming and cheering erupted outside the door, signaling the band's arrival. The door burst open and everyone but Samantha rushed in. "Hi, honey," Ruby called brightly as she and the others were ushered through onto the plane by one of Lisa's assistants. While Julia continued talking with Adele, her heart began pounding as she waited for Samantha to come through the door.

A few minutes later, she walked in, with Lisa right behind her. Samantha glanced around quickly, and when she saw Julia she stopped, her look intense and intimate, sending tremors pulsing through Julia's body. She found it hard to concentrate on what Adele was saying. She held Samantha's gaze and saw her expression transform into a friendly smile, then she left with Lisa to board the aircraft. Julia finished her phone conversation and waited for Kerry to come through.

Ten minutes later, Julia inched her way up the aisle, Kerry behind her, and she could see Samantha already seated on the aisle a few rows ahead of her. Julia hoped Samantha would look up, but she didn't. When Julia came alongside her, she saw Samantha was staring at a magazine open on her lap. She seemed to be studying it with great concentration, but it was only a full-page photo of an Australian Airlines plane against a clear blue sky, and she had to smile to herself.

They were inches apart, and Julia was sure Samantha could feel the electricity between them too. She looked at Samantha's shining, golden blond hair and ached to touch it. Don was sitting beside her, and Julia smiled at him before moving on.

Julia fastened her seatbelt, as the plane began take-off. "Do you think it'll still be hot in Brisbane?" Kerry asked.

"Oh, yeah, hotter than Sydney anyway."

Lisa, sitting behind them, leaned over the backs of their seats. "Don't forget, you two, we've got a special dinner organized tonight at the hotel with all the heavies from B.G.I. It should be good." Julia inwardly groaned. She'd forgotten about the dinner. There would be little chance of talking privately with Samantha tonight. "My boss is looking forward to meeting you, Julia."

"Oh, that's nice." Julia hoped her smile was pleasant. Meeting with a B.G.I. executive tonight was the last thing she wanted.

An hour later, at two o'clock, they landed in Brisbane. It was warm, around eighty degrees, and quite humid. Straight after they arrived at their hotel,

Kerry went off with the others to look at the Lyric Theater where the concerts would be held. Julia declined Ruby's invitation to join them. It would be a strain being in Samantha's company while she was maintaining this distant attitude. At reception, she arranged to have the city newspaper, *The Courier Mail*, delivered to her each morning, in order to keep up with the articles and reviews that would appear about Samantha. Then she headed for her room.

She sighed with relief as she closed her door. Opening the double doors onto the balcony, she surveyed the view of the city and the Brisbane River. She felt tired — she hadn't been sleeping well — and decided to rest for a few minutes. She pulled off her jeans and shirt and lay down on the bed. A soothing breeze from the open doors cooled her perspiring skin.

She slowly regained consciousness as the insistent ring of the phone penetrated her brain. Disoriented, she glanced at the clock on the bedside console. It was five-thirty. She'd been asleep for three hours.

"Hi," Lisa said. "I wanted to let you know that dinner's in the Globe Room downstairs at seven-thirty."

"Oh, okay, thanks," Julia mumbled sleepily.

"I have to pass your room. I'll come by and pick you up on the way."

Lisa hung up before she could protest. She wasn't interested in going to the dinner with Lisa — she wasn't interested in the dinner at all. But at least she could see Samantha, and maybe Samantha wouldn't avoid her all night.

By the time she had a shower, Julia felt bright and rejuvenated from her nap and optimistic about seeing Samantha. Persistent, erotic thoughts engulfed her as she put on her cocktail dress — a classic black dress with fine shoulder straps, low-cut, short but not too short, and fitted to her shape with a zipper up the back. Julia thought it was elegant and sexy, and she hoped Samantha would think so.

She clipped on a delicate gold necklace with tiny emeralds and small, matching earrings. She spritzed on perfume and heard Lisa's knock just as she finished applying her rose-pink lipstick. She slipped on her black high-heeled court shoes, grabbed her purse and went to the door.

"Hi, Lisa." Julia began to step through the doorway but Lisa put her hand on Julia's arm gently, stopping her.

"Hey, there's no hurry," she said with a smile. "I thought we'd have a drink first."

Julia reluctantly found herself moving aside as Lisa came in, closing the door behind her. "It's seven-thirty. Shouldn't we go downstairs? Everyone'll be there."

"Oh, they'll be standing around drinking and chatting for ages. We've got time."

Julia was anxious to see Samantha, but Lisa had put her into a position where she would have to be rude to get her out of there, and Julia didn't want to do that. She liked Lisa. Smiling, hoping to cover her impatience, she went to the bar fridge. "What would you like?"

"A beer, please." Julia could feel Lisa's eyes on her as she got the beer and a glass of mineral water for herself. She reached for a glass to pour the beer.

"The bottle's fine." Lisa twisted off the cap and said, "I like your dress."

"Thank you." Julia sipped her Perrier. Lisa's gaze

was unsettling. "We should hurry. Your boss will be looking for you."

Lisa glanced down at Julia's cleavage. "Am I making you nervous?"

"No, of course not." Julia looked directly at Lisa and gave what she hoped was an ordinary, friendly smile. Lisa was being more flirtatious than usual, and it occurred to Julia that if Lisa were a man, Julia would be feeling extremely nervous and uncomfortable right about then, alone in this room. But she found the attention flattering, even if it was unwanted.

Lisa took a swig of beer and set the bottle down on the coffee table. She sauntered over to Julia, who was still standing by the bar. She stroked Julia's arm softly with one finger. "I'm very attracted to you, Julia. Maybe you've noticed."

Julia was glad her glass was on the counter, or she would have dropped it. She hadn't expected Lisa to make such an overt pass at her. She swallowed. "Thank you, Lisa, but —"

"There's someone else on your mind, perhaps?"

Julia nodded, picked up her glass and took a drink.

Lisa gave a resigned kind of smile. "I wonder who she could be," she said with gentle irony. Julia wasn't sure how to respond. She gave a slight shrug. Lisa remained as warm and friendly as usual. "Well, I don't know that I should be overly concerned. After all, she's not here, is she?"

Julia stared down into her glass. She wished that Samantha *was* here — that she was going to the dinner with her.

Lisa strolled to the door. "We'd better go."

As Julia picked up her purse and headed for the door, she thought how much more pleasant women were about these things. In her experience, men had always taken a knock-back badly, becoming cool or sulky, or worse. She also noted that as far as Lisa was concerned, Julia was a dyke, and that pleased her immensely.

Samantha was surrounded by a group of gushing women — the wives and girlfriends of the mostly male executives from B.G.I. She was doing her best to entertain them, but she was on edge, waiting for Julia.

They had exchanged a glance in the hotel lobby that afternoon when they arrived, and the obvious passion in Julia's expression made Samantha tingle. Then Julia had gone upstairs to her room.

She was worried Julia was hurt about last night, or angry. She knew she should just leave things alone, but her desire was in constant battle with her common sense.

Suddenly, the door opened and Samantha froze in mid-sentence as she watched Julia enter the room. She was stunning. Lisa came in behind her, and with her hand at Julia's back, she introduced her to a B.G.I. executive. With a toss of her chestnut hair, Julia gave a charming smile and shook the guy's hand. Samantha was shaken for a moment by the memory of that soft, perfumed hair against her face — that one heavenly time when she allowed herself to hold Julia in her arms. It seemed like a lifetime ago. The man left, and

Lisa moved close to Julia, whispering something to her. Samantha couldn't stand it.

She turned back to the women before her. "I'm sorry. You'll have to excuse me for a moment."

She quickly crossed the room toward Julia, as Lisa, thankfully, left her side. Samantha was tongue-tied, mesmerized by the sight of her. Julia seemed composed, exhibiting a self-assurance that was unnerving. She wasn't saying anything, and Samantha felt totally off-balance. Her heart began to pound, and in an attempt to save herself, she broke eye contact, only to find herself staring at Julia's exposed cleavage, which didn't help. Samantha swallowed hard, then looked directly into Julia's glowing, emerald eyes. "You're not angry with me, are you?"

Julia gave her hair a sexy little toss. "No. Not angry." Her voice sounded husky, breathless.

All Samantha could think of was taking Julia into her arms, right there, and kissing her. The rest of the room was a blur.

"Hi, Samantha," said Lisa, making Samantha jump. Lisa placed her hand on Julia's back again and began to steer her away. "They're serving dinner. I think we should go and sit down now."

Samantha stood there impotently, as Julia, with one parting, seductive glance, allowed herself to be led away.

"Over here, Sam," Ruby called, indicating a seat beside her.

Beautifully presented platters were being placed on the table. There were lobsters, prawns, oysters, salads, hot chili mud-crabs and spicy noodle dishes. Waiters were bustling around filling wine glasses. Samantha sat down but kept glancing at Julia at the opposite end of the table.

Julia was smiling and chatting, looking gorgeous. She had those business executives eating out of her hand. Lisa had her arm draped over the back of Julia's chair and was leaning close to her.

Samantha felt a huge pang of jealousy and she quietly muttered to Ruby, "Will you take a look at Lisa, for Christ's sake? She's all over Julia — it's pathetic."

Ruby glanced at Lisa, then chuckled as she helped herself to some lobster. "She's just doing what you wish you were doing, honey, that's all."

Samantha was battling with herself. She had a choice. If she wasn't prepared to get involved with Julia, then it wasn't her business what Julia did with anyone else. But it was hard to resist the urge to go over and grab her, get her out of the room, away from Lisa, where they could be alone.

She drank some wine and took a serving of chili crab. "Well, Lisa can hit on her as much as she likes — she's wasting her time. Julia wouldn't sleep with her."

"Not while you're around, honey. She's crazy about you." Ruby gave Lisa a speculative look. Apparently lost in her thoughts, Ruby seemed to forget herself, then in her usual bright, loud voice, she said, "But in the right mood I'd probably sleep with her if she asked. Hard and fast, I reckon she'd be."

Ruby's voice seemed to ricochet around the room. "Jesus, Ruby," Samantha breathed, as she cringed and stared down at the table. The conversation close by them seemed to halt and she could hear Kerry, sitting opposite, snickering quietly.

Samantha slowly raised her head and found herself gazing across the table directly into the startled, china-blue eyes of a young blond woman. Her forkful of noodles hovered tremulously in midair, and her huge diamond engagement ring glittered virtuously.

"Is everything okay?" Samantha hoped her smile looked warm and reassuring. "Are you having a good time?" The woman nodded vaguely, and looked away.

"Oops," Ruby whispered, and they both broke up into choking, stifled laughter. Ruby recovered and drank some water. "You've gotta stop torturing yourself, Sam. Once Julia's out there, women are gonna be queuing up for her, honey. She is one pretty girl and you can't blame Lisa for trying. You're gonna be on the other side of the world in a few days, and you won't know a thing about it." Ruby sipped her wine. "Of course, if you weren't so stubborn, things might be different."

Samantha pushed her plate away. She'd lost her appetite. "It's impossible."

"Imperfect, honey."

"Impossible, Ruby."

Ruby chuckled. "That's the same thing to you, ain't it, girl."

The rest of the dinner was difficult. Samantha made small talk, and when at last the table was being cleared and everyone was moving around the room talking, drinking coffee and liqueurs, Samantha was relieved. Julia, she noted, was engaged in conversation with one person after another, with Lisa constantly by her side.

Kerry, Ruby and the other band members decided to go out to a nightclub, but Samantha was in no mood to join them. She desperately wanted to talk to

Julia but knew any attempt at ordinary, friendly conversation was useless. It was painful just to be there watching her. Now and then, Julia caught her eye, which rendered Samantha helpless by the passion in her glance. And each time Lisa touched her, Samantha's fists clenched in anguish.

CHAPTER TEN

It was only eleven o'clock and Samantha wasn't ready for sleep. Despondent and tense, she didn't know what to do with herself except pour a large glass of bourbon. She picked up a novel she'd started but couldn't concentrate on it. The idea of a bubble bath suddenly appealed. There was a TV in the large bathroom and she could relax for a while and watch a movie.

Five minutes after she'd settled in with a bourbon in one hand and the remote control in the other, there was a knock at her door. "For Christ's sake," she grumbled as she got out of the tub and wrapped herself in a towel. If it was Danny, she thought, she'd tell him to come back later.

"Who is it?"

"Julia." Samantha's heart leapt at the sound of her voice and without another thought, she opened the door. Her heart began to race as she looked at her, standing there in that sexy dress, her eyes blazing, her expression determined. Julia slowly looked her up and down and, with a confident toss of her hair, she said quietly, "Aren't you going to ask me in?" Samantha felt her throat tighten, and without a word, she stood aside.

Julia made no move to sit down, but rather stood just inside the door, gazing at her.

With difficulty, Samantha found her voice. "I'll just go and get dressed." She turned toward the bathroom, but Julia reached out and grabbed her towel. Samantha gasped and clutched it tightly to her breasts, but Julia held on. She stepped out of her high heels. Helpless, Samantha quivered as desire pumped through her body. She closed her eyes for a moment, and the towel fell to the floor.

Suddenly, Julia was in her arms, kissing her passionately, her hands gliding over her slippery skin. Samantha was on fire. Julia's hands slid down over her hips, moving around to the front of her thighs, and when Julia's mouth moved to her breasts, her tongue flickering across her nipples, Samantha thought she'd collapse.

She caught Julia's wrists and, holding her close, unzipped her dress and pulled it down to her hips. Oh, God, she thought. A scanty half-cup, black lace bra . . . leave it. It offered a teasing glimpse of taut, rosy pink nipples and was so sexy Samantha's head swam. Julia was trembling. She should go slowly, she thought as she kissed Julia's perfumed shoulders. It was Julia's first time. She kissed Julia's throat, then trailed her tongue down into her cleavage. Julia gasped. Samantha ran her fingers across one breast and gently squeezed the nipple between her fingers. Julia shuddered and murmured incoherently.

God! She *couldn't* go slowly.

Julia felt the bed bounce as she fell back, and Samantha was on top of her. Samantha's mouth consumed her. Samantha broke contact for a moment to drag Julia's clothes off, then her mouth was at Julia's breasts — her tongue tracing along the edge of her bra, her teeth gently teasing Julia's swollen nipples through the lace. Julia clasped Samantha's shoulders tightly as her lust increased.

Samantha's fingers were trailing up the inside of her thigh, leaving a fiery wake, and then she stroked her — just once between her thighs. Julia gasped. Suddenly, Samantha's fingers thrust inside her. Julia groaned, closed her eyes, felt her hips rise. Samantha's fingers plunged more deeply. Her mind went blank as a powerful heat pumped through her body. She couldn't stop gasping. She reached down to feel Samantha's hand, her wet fingers thrusting into her, then they withdrew a little and stilled, applying pressure inside her, her thumb outside, stroking her.

Julia felt herself rising to a peak of electrifying

tension that was surpassed again and again. It was as if she were flying at an incredible speed through a dark night to a place she'd never been.

She opened her eyes slowly and Samantha was gazing at her, the muscles of her face taut, her eyes dark and passionate, misted with tears. "Yes, baby," Samantha whispered.

Julia closed her eyes again, and piercing white lights replaced the darkness. She felt her body open, and an incredible wetness flowed from her. She grasped Samantha's shoulders again as powerful contractions shook her.

As the tremors gradually slowed, she watched Samantha kissing her breasts. She ran her fingers through Samantha's silky hair; Samantha's body was trembling against hers.

Blissful and sweet melancholy welled inside her. Julia felt tears trickling down her cheeks. They lay still for a while, holding each other. Samantha kissed away her tears, Julia stroked her back, and she could feel Samantha's heart pounding. Julia took Samantha's face in her hands and kissed her. She wanted to touch Samantha and kiss her all over, but she was hesitant. She didn't know what Samantha expected. She trailed her fingers around to Samantha's breasts and stroked one light pink nipple. Samantha quivered. With a rush of passion, she turned Samantha onto her back and she yielded with a soft sigh. Julia's heart was thumping. She wished she knew what to do. She began to kiss Samantha's throat and shoulders and breasts, her skin like satin under her tongue. She placed herself between Samantha's legs and felt Samantha's wetness against her stomach. Slowly, she kissed her way down across Samantha's stomach, closer to her hips. She wanted to go further — to be as intimate as she could be — to kiss Samantha between her thighs, caress her with her tongue. But she was apprehensive. She assumed Samantha would like that, but she was unsure how to go about it. She didn't want to disappoint her.

Samantha's breathing became ragged, and with each exhale, she groaned quietly. Samantha caressed Julia's face, ran her fingers through her hair, and her touch was reassuring. Julia traced her tongue along the sensitive skin at the crease of her thighs. Samantha's hips writhed and she made a whimpering sound. Encouraged, Julia brought her mouth to her, breathed in the heady, pungent scent, then in wonder at the complex, salty taste, tentatively stroked with her tongue. Samantha groaned. A wave of lust overwhelmed her and Julia trembled as she pressed her mouth into the wet heat of Samantha's desire. Samantha's hands were in Julia's hair, holding her head, guiding her, as Julia, finding her rhythm, feasted.

The line between giving and taking had vanished. Giving pleasure to Samantha felt almost selfish. Julia moaned at the thought as she bathed her mouth in Samantha's passion. Her earlier concern about being able to satisfy Samantha disappeared, and she felt like she had been waiting for this moment all her life.

She held Samantha's hips firmly, feeling the tension building in Samantha's body, and she shuddered with a surge of desire as she felt Samantha's first fluttering contractions against her mouth.

When Samantha cried out and arched her hips, Julia felt Samantha's powerful tremors flow through her and knew she was in love with Samantha.

The next morning, Samantha, fast asleep, lay close beside her. Desire stirred, and Julia was overtaken by a delicious lassitude. She felt perfectly happy. She glanced at the clock beside the bed and, with a jolt, saw that it was already eight-thirty. Samantha had a rehearsal at ten, and Julia also had a busy day planned.

Samantha looked so peaceful, Julia couldn't bear to wake her just yet, so she got up quietly. She smiled when she saw the state of the bed. Sheets had come adrift, blankets and pillows had fallen to the floor. Samantha had only a corner of the sheet draped across her, and she'd fallen asleep without even a pillow under her head.

Julia slipped on one of the hotel's bath robes, rang room service and ordered breakfast. She carefully covered Samantha with the rest of the sheet without disturbing her. While she waited for breakfast to arrive, she sat on the balcony, watching the commuter ferries traveling back and forth across the river.

Breakfast was delivered and set up on the table on the balcony. As the waiter was leaving the room, Samantha stirred, and he glanced from Samantha to Julia, his young face reddening slightly, and Julia smiled as she closed the door behind him.

She went to Samantha and, taking her in her arms, kissed her. Samantha moaned sleepily and returned the kiss passionately. She began to drag Julia back into bed.

Reluctantly, Julia said, "We have to get up, darling. It's late. I've got breakfast ready for you."

Samantha released her with a groan of disappointment, rubbed her eyes and, pulling on a robe, followed Julia out onto the balcony. The table was spread with a platter of sliced paw-paw, mango and pineapple, a basket of warm croissants and a pot of coffee.

Samantha was quiet and sat looking at Julia, smiling her sexy, special smile, her eyes filled with an erotic intimacy that made Julia tingle.

Julia poured their coffee and they ate in comfortable silence. Samantha took Julia's legs onto her lap and stroked them while she sipped her coffee and gazed at her. Julia felt desire pulsing through her. It was difficult to suppress, but she finally stood and kissed Samantha's cheek. "It's nine-fifteen, darling. I'd better get dressed and go to my room, and you'd better have a shower."

"In a minute, baby."

Samantha drew Julia down onto her lap and began to kiss her. Her fingers crept along Julia's thigh, under the robe, teasing her. Pulling the robe open, she nuzzled her face into Julia's breasts. "You smell of sex and Chanel," she murmured. "What a combination."

Julia couldn't restrain her lust any longer. She straddled Samantha's knees. Her heart was pounding and she was breathless. Instantly, Samantha's fingers found her and Julia gasped, laying her head on Samantha's shoulder as she rode her fingers. The fire within her heightened quickly and fiercely until Julia felt her whole body dissolve, then she was shaking; her contractions held Samantha tightly, deeply, inside her.

The piercing white lights behind her eyelids were slowly replaced by the bright, glinting sunlight on the river as she opened her eyes, and Samantha was softly biting her shoulder. Julia sighed.

She reached down inside Samantha's robe but Samantha took her hand and kissed it. "There's no time, honey. I've gotta go."

Julia washed her face and, borrowing Samantha's comb, tidied her hair. She laughed as she picked up her crumpled dress from the floor and put it on. "I hope I don't pass anyone on the way to my room. It's pretty obvious what I was up to last night."

Samantha laughed too, but when she held Julia close and kissed her goodbye, Julia could see tears in her eyes. When she asked anxiously what was wrong, Samantha just shook her head and bit her lip.

Julia felt she could understand the tears. She was so overwhelmed by her own emotions, she constantly felt on the verge of tears herself. "I'll come to the concert, then see you back here later. My room, okay?"

Samantha held her tightly and kissed her again, and Julia could feel Samantha's tears on her face. "Goodbye, baby," Samantha whispered.

CHAPTER ELEVEN

"For God's sake, Louis, can't you get that intro right? That bass melody line has gotta be fucking perfect, so I harmonize with it when I come in!" Samantha pushed her hair back off her forehead impatiently. Stunned, Louis was staring at her. She yelled at him, "How many fucking times do we have to do this?"

"Samantha!" Ruby sounded terse. "He did it right the last two times. You got it wrong! You came in half a bar early."

"Oh, right! So now I don't know how to sing my

117

own goddamn songs!" The place was hot and stifling. She dragged off her sweater and threw it across to one side of the stage. "Let's just forget the whole fucking thing! Where's Danny? It was his stupid idea to do this." She knew he was around somewhere talking to the sound mixer. "Danny!" she shouted.

Danny appeared out of the darkness and stood at the foot of the stage. "Yeah?"

"We're not doing that other song. It's a pain in the ass. We're just wasting fucking time."

"Whatcha talkin' about, Sam? It's the perfect opportunity to introduce another song off the album — the last single's gettin' tired. You know I'm tryin' to push another one onto the charts, keep up the momentum. What's your problem?"

Samantha felt her throat tighten; tears were pricking at her eyes. Her mind was in turmoil. She was bursting with such a confusing mixture of emotions that she felt out of control. She bit her lip and shrugged.

"The problem is we need to take a lunch break." Ruby's voice was tight.

Danny stroked his sleek hair in quick, agitated movements. "So, whatcha tellin' me for? Take a goddamn lunch break, for Christ's sake! Is that it?"

"Yeah, honey, that's it. The song'll be fine."

Danny shook his head and disappeared back into the darkness, muttering to himself. Ruby was glaring at her angrily and Samantha sank down onto a box at the side of the stage. She watched Louis, Don and Jenny silently unplug their instruments and walk off.

"See y'all back here in an hour." Ruby came and stood in front of her. She crossed her arms, and her bangles pealed like warning bells. "So, what's the matter with you, girl! You're acting like the bitch from hell!"

Samantha couldn't hold back the tide any longer, and sinking her face into her hands, she burst into tears. Ruby sat beside her and put her arm around her. "I'm in love with her, Ruby. I spent last night with her and now I'm completely gone . . . I knew this would happen." She wiped at her tears impatiently. "I'm so confused . . . I don't know what to do."

To her amazement, Ruby laughed gently. "Oh, my, now ain't that a surprise!" She chuckled again. "Well, honey, what most people do when they fall in love is, they feel real happy about it and make exciting plans and stuff like that."

"What? Feel happy until Sunday? Four whole goddamn days? Don't you get it, Ruby? We can't make plans! I've fallen in love with the most wonderful and beautiful woman I've ever met and I've gotta give her up!" She stood up and paced back and forth across the stage.

"No, you don't."

Samantha felt like exploding in frustration. "Oh, right! I'll fucking emigrate, will I? I'll just stroll on down to the embassy this afternoon and get it all organized, will I?" She glared at Ruby, who looked unimpressed.

"If you're both in love, you'll figure out some way to make it work. You might have to compromise a little, honey."

"Compromise? Like what? See her for a few weeks, a few times a year? Don't you think I've thought about all that?" She bit her lip to prevent the tears from overcoming her again. "This isn't some nice little affair! I've never loved anyone like this! It'd be agony every day that I wasn't with her." She kicked at an amplifier lead that was lying on the floor.

"So, it's all or nothing, as usual."

Samantha shook her head in exasperation. "It's impossible! It would kill me to have a part-time relationship with her. I can't compromise."

"Of course not," Ruby said dryly. "Let's go get some lunch."

It was early evening and Julia and Kerry were having dinner together at the brasserie opposite their hotel on the other side of the river. They were seated at an outdoor table overlooking the water. The evening was warm and Julia was conscious of the way the gentle breeze caressed her skin. The river was a complex fusion of greens and blues with ever-changing lights and shadows that she hadn't noticed before, and the first streaks of the setting sun behind the sparse clouds were brilliantly red and orange. She finished her gnocchi and salad, surprised at how good the simple meal tasted.

She glanced again across at the hotel, and thought Samantha would be back there by now. She'd be having something to eat, then dressing for the concert. She wondered what she was eating, what she'd be wearing. She felt her body ripple gently, like the river in the breeze.

She sighed contentedly and sipped her wine. Kerry was gazing at the water, drinking her beer. The fading sun shone through the glass and cast an amber light on Kerry's face. The tiny spikes of her cropped, fair hair glistened, and the sunlight exposed the vulnerable, pink skin of her temples. She was wearing a bright-red satin shirt which, Julia thought, was quite a change from her usual muted checks.

Julia smiled. "I like your shirt."

Kerry grinned. "Ruby bought it for me when we went shopping one day in Sydney. It was expensive and I tried to say no, but Ruby said, 'Don't be silly, honey. Just take the goddamn thing — it suits you.' " They both laughed at Kerry's impression of Ruby's accent.

"Is there something going on between you two?"

Kerry sighed. "No, worst luck. I think she's stunning and so cool, but she just mothers me." Kerry began drawing patterns in the condensation on her glass. "What about you?" She stole a shy glance at Julia. "I, um, couldn't help noticing you and Samantha last week — you know, dancing and everything."

Julia smiled happily. "Yes. There's most definitely something going on with us."

"Shit! I thought you were straight."

"I guess I did, too, but wondered why I wasn't very good at it."

Clearly impressed, Kerry shook her head incredulously. "Unreal! Samantha Knight! She's the most gorgeous woman in the universe!"

Julia laughed. "I wouldn't argue with that."

"What's going to happen when she goes home?"

Julia finished her wine. "We haven't figured that out yet. We've got a lot to talk about, but it'll work out somehow. I know that much." She glanced at her watch. "God, it's seven-fifteen. We'd better go back and get ready for the concert."

Upstairs, Julia rang room service and ordered a bottle of vintage Moët et Chandon and two glasses to be delivered to her room later in the evening.

While she showered and dressed, she looked forward to the concert. Last time she watched Samantha perform, she'd glanced at Julia quickly, expressionless, but this concert would be different. When Samantha looked at her tonight, it would be with the exciting, seductive, intimacy of a lover.

She planned to tell Samantha tonight that she was in love with her. Maybe it was too soon to be saying things like that, but there was no time to be coy. She'd never said those words to anyone before and she prayed Samantha would feel the same. Instinctively, she felt Samantha loved her. Later, after they'd made love, they'd talk about the future.

She put on a deep emerald-green fitted silk dress with a matching long, loose jacket, the gold earrings and high heels. She sprayed on her perfume and was just applying her dusky-beige lipstick, when there was a knock at her door.

She was surprised when a valet handed her a huge box of flowers. "The house-keeper will come and arrange them for you later, madam," he said with a smile, as Julia tipped him.

She closed the door and opened the box. It was filled with the most exquisite irises she'd ever seen. They were a perfect, breathtaking blue, and there were at least four dozen of them. A sealed envelope lay on top of the stems. She tore it open eagerly.

She couldn't believe her eyes — she thought she'd pass out. Her heart was pounding and the knot in her stomach felt like lead. She sank down onto a chair and read the note over and over. Tears began to flow down her cheeks, dripping onto the note in her hand. The ink smudged and blurred and her head swam. This just wasn't possible.

She jumped at the ring of the phone. Sick and disoriented, she rose slowly to answer it.

"I've been waiting in the lobby for you for ten minutes, Julia. We'll be late if we don't leave now." Kerry's voice sounded distant and muffled against the deafening pulse in her ears.

"Um, I can't go. You go on without me."

"You sound strange. What's wrong?"

"Nothing. Just go, okay?"

Julia went to the fridge and took out a bottle of wine. Her hand shook as she poured the first glass. She drank it quickly and poured another. She sat down again and reread the note.

Dear Julia,

I didn't know how else to do this. I hope you'll understand. I wish with all my heart that things didn't have to be this way, but our lives are in different places — so far apart. There's no future for us. It's already going to be hard enough for me to get on that plane on Sunday — leaving you — but if I spend these last days with you, it'll be unbearable. I think it's best that we don't see each other alone again. That would only make things more difficult. I have to get on with my life, and you have to get on with yours. So I'm saying goodbye now.

You're the most beautiful woman I've ever known,

and I know you'll meet a woman someday soon who'll make you as happy as you deserve to be. I hope, in the longer term, we can be friends.

I'll never forget you.

Samantha.

Backstage, Samantha was jumpy. She poured herself her fourth glass of bourbon. The painful ache in her chest was getting worse and the bourbon wasn't helping. She was made-up, ready to go onstage, but no matter how hard she tried, the tears kept welling up and she had to keep dabbing her eyes with a tissue to keep them from pouring down her face. She had such a lump in her throat that she wondered how she'd be able to sing.

"Don't drink that, honey, we go on in ten minutes."

Samantha could hear the opening act starting their last song. The thought of going out there tonight filled her with dread. She kept picturing Julia, reading her note, and she felt sick at the thought of how hurt Julia would be. She knew when she decided to end things this way, that it'd be hard. But it would save more pain later, she kept telling herself. She gulped down the bourbon. *God, how could it get any worse than this?* She said, "Do you think she'll understand, Ruby?"

Ruby was still looking stunned by what Samantha had just told her, and she shook her head incredulously. "I can't believe you actually gave her the kiss-off! Not Julia!" She sighed. "And no, I don't think she'll understand. I sure don't!"

This wasn't making her feel any better. "Would it have been better to wait until we were at the goddamn airport? Then say, ' 'Bye, honey. See you in six months or a year. Don't forget to write.' Would that be easier? After we'd had more time to get closer and for me to love her even more?"

Ruby shrugged sadly. "I don't know."

"See? There's no other way! I can't go around letting things just happen and having no direction. You've gotta take control of your life or everything ends up in a huge mess."

"Oh, yeah, honey. I can see that! I'm real impressed with your damage-control techniques."

Samantha sighed impatiently. It was no use trying to make Ruby understand. "Will you call her when we get back to the hotel? Talk to her and make her understand, make her feel better?"

"It won't be me she'll wanna talk to." In the background, the audience broke into applause as the band finished their act. "Come on, fix your face. We've gotta go on."

"Will you, Ruby?"

"Yeah, honey, I'll call her." She took Samantha's arm. "Come here. Look at you, for Christ's sake." She grabbed some makeup from the table and began sponging more foundation onto Samantha's face, removing the mascara smudges from under her eyes. "Now, put on your lipstick, girl. There's women in those back rows with goddamn binoculars."

Danny raced into the room with a beaming smile. "Okay, guys, go out there and kill 'em!"

A minute later, Samantha was standing in the spotlight while the crowd erupted into wild screaming and rapturous applause, and the show was on.

* * * * *

Julia had finished the bottle of wine. Light-headed, she stood to answer the knock at her door. She realized she'd been sitting in the dark and flicked on a lamp. The flowers, arranged in a vase by a housemaid earlier, were suddenly illuminated. Shaken, she quickly averted her eyes.

Room service had arrived with the champagne. The waiter set down the tray on the table. The bottle was standing in a silver ice bucket, surrounded by crushed ice. Two elegant, fluted glasses stood alongside. He smiled and was about to leave.

"Could you open it and pour it, please."

He shot a quick, subtle glance around the room, as if looking for her companion, then smiled again. "Certainly, madam." He filled the two glasses and left, and Julia took them both over to the coffee table by the sofa.

She drank her glass of champagne, and wondered how she could have gotten it so wrong. Thank God she hadn't told Samantha she loved her. Samantha — a beautiful, talented woman, adored by literally millions of women. How many times had Samantha been told that?

She drank Samantha's glass of champagne and decided her problem was that she was a novice at this love game. She'd actually thought Samantha loved her too.

She poured another glass. She was sure, though, that Samantha really cared for her. She just *knew* that, and couldn't figure out why Samantha didn't want to discuss the situation with her. Perhaps Samantha was worried that Julia would want too much. She drained the glass and considered ruefully that if Samantha thought that, she was probably right. Julia was in love with her, and she wanted it all.

By the time she finished the bottle, she felt calmer. Her senses were dulled. She decided she had to get out of that room — she was suffocating.

She washed her face and reapplied her makeup. She had no idea of where to go, but she didn't want to be around when Samantha returned within an hour or so.

She went downstairs and, on impulse, headed into the small, quiet bar. There were only a few couples whispering intimately, and the soft light and classical music were soothing. She ordered a glass of brandy and wished there was someone who could tell her it would all be okay. But there was no one she knew who would understand her love for Samantha, let alone the pain she was feeling. She wanted to talk to Samantha, only to her, but Samantha clearly didn't want that.

She finished her second brandy and looked at her watch. She had to blink to focus; her head was spinning a little. It was ten-thirty and Samantha would be back soon. She had to think of somewhere to go. She twirled the empty glass and watched it glint in the lamplight.

Suddenly, she was angry. She should confront Samantha and demand to know how she could do this — how she could just walk away. But she knew if she set eyes on Samantha, it wouldn't be that way. She wouldn't be dignified. She'd be pathetic. She'd probably fall at Samantha's feet, sobbing helplessly, telling her she loved her and adored her.

"Can I get you a refill?"

Julia jumped, surprised to see Lisa. She panicked. "Is the concert over? Are they back?" She was conscious of the tears in her eyes.

"No, I left early." Lisa ordered another brandy and a scotch, then took the empty glass from Julia and held her hand. She stroked the back of Julia's hand with her thumb. It felt warm and comforting. "You've been crying. Has Samantha upset you?"

Julia had been fighting the tears, but Lisa's gentle tone weakened her, and she was suddenly overwhelmed. She felt the room spin for a moment as Lisa drew her to her feet. She held Julia tightly as she led her out of the bar and up to Lisa's room.

"It's okay," Lisa said softly. Julia's tears had subsided and she sank gratefully into an armchair. Lisa got her a glass of cold water, and Julia felt the haze lift slightly. She should go back to her room soon, she thought. She'd be able to sleep now.

She leaned her head back against the chair. She hadn't told Lisa anything. How could she tell her she was in love with Samantha. She'd surely laugh and say, "Yeah, you and every other dyke in the world!" Samantha had so much charm and seductiveness that perhaps, Julia thought, she'd misread Samantha's feelings for her. Fortunately, Lisa wasn't demanding an explanation for her tears. In fact, she was being very sympathetic.

Lisa returned from the bathroom with a cool, damp face cloth, and she knelt beside Julia's chair and began to gently wipe her hot, tear-stained face. Julia sighed and closed her eyes. It felt good.

She felt a soft caress on her cheek, and she sighed again. A feathery kiss lit on her cheek, then on her throat, and she felt her body stir. Lisa kissed her mouth and Julia moaned. Sensual memories filled her mind. She pictured Samantha lying back, watching Julia with dark eyes, as she explored Samantha's body with warm, slow kisses. In her mind, she heard Samantha gasp when she touched her.

When Lisa kissed her again, passionately, Julia felt a powerful surge of lust. She put her arms around Lisa and murmured, "Hold me."

The room spun again as Lisa held her and undressed her. Julia felt hot — she wanted her clothes off quickly. She was in a hurry.

The cool sheet against her skin was a relief. Her mind was empty of everything but her urgent need. Her breasts felt heavy and her nipples ached for the warm, wet caress that soon came, as Lisa kissed them. Julia saw Samantha's gorgeous face in her mind so clearly she could almost touch her.

She felt her thighs being parted. Lisa was stroking her, sending erotic charges through her body. Julia gripped the sheet and held on tightly. She was out of control, like she was floating away. Then Lisa's fingers penetrated her and Julia groaned and writhed as the pressure built within her. She felt a soft warmth between her thighs and imagined it was Samantha's silky hair brushing against her skin.

Suddenly, the moment of release ripped through her, and she lay there shaking, gasping for breath. She was in a daze.

She heard a tiny cry — she thought it must have been her own. Then she realized in a shocking, crystallized moment that the cry was from Lisa, who collapsed beside her, shaking and shining with perspiration.

Lisa held her, stroking her cheek, but Julia

couldn't respond to her or even look at her. She turned her face away and tears rolled down her cheeks as her body throbbed with an odious gratification. Soon, she slipped into a deep sleep.

"For Christ's sake, Ruby, it's two o'clock in the goddamn morning! Where on earth could she be?" Samantha was pacing up and down in Ruby's room.

Ruby had been phoning Julia's room repeatedly for about two hours and she had gone and knocked on her door several times. The hotel confirmed Julia had accepted a delivery of flowers at around seven forty-five and hadn't handed in her key.

"Like I said, she simply must've gone out somewhere, honey, and forgotten to drop in her key."

"But where the hell would she go?" Samantha poured herself another bourbon. "She's not the type to just disappear without leaving anyone a message. It doesn't make any sense." She gulped her drink.

"What did you expect her to do? Read your letter, then settle down comfortably and watch a movie, or something?" Ruby shrugged. "Maybe she's checked into another hotel for the night, to avoid you."

Samantha's heart was pounding and she felt sick with worry. Tears began to flow down her face. "I just wanna know she's all right. I can't stand not knowing where she is, what's happened to her." Ruby put her arms around her and Samantha broke down.

"She'll be fine, honey. Don't worry."

"I didn't think she'd do anything crazy. I knew she'd be hurt, the same as me, but I thought she'd see the sense of what I said."

"Maybe she does. But maybe she's angry too." Ruby patted her back comfortingly and Samantha wiped away her tears.

"I couldn't bear it if she hated me for this. I hoped that by Sunday, we might've been able to say goodbye as friends."

"Shit! You don't want much, do you, girl."

Samantha withdrew from Ruby's arms and poured herself another drink. She suddenly pictured Julia's face and a terrible pain tore at her heart. She longed to have her in her arms again. "Maybe I shouldn't have sent the note." She turned to Ruby, suddenly shaken with panic. "Maybe I should've left things alone!"

Ruby's eyes widened in feigned horror. "What! And let things take their own course? Why, honey, then you would've had to discuss it all with the woman you love and let her take some control, and we couldn't have that, now could we?"

Samantha bit her lip, fighting against more tears. Her mind was a muddle of self-doubt battling with conviction.

Ruby took the glass from her hand. "Everything'll look better in the morning," she said gently. "Julia's probably fast asleep right now, in some hotel downtown, and she'll be back tomorrow." She led Samantha to the door and kissed her cheek. "Go get some sleep, honey, there's nothing more you can do tonight, except drive yourself mad."

The clock beside the bed read three o'clock. Julia's head was aching and her mouth was dry. A cool breeze blowing in through the open balcony doors made her shiver.

Lisa, asleep beside her, was breathing deeply and evenly. With a feeling of increasing despair, Julia recalled the events of the night. She carefully moved out from under Lisa's arm and thigh. Lisa stirred and turned over without waking. Julia found her clothes and dressed quickly in the darkness, then tiptoed out.

CHAPTER TWELVE

The blue irises stood majestically in a tall glass vase on the desk under the window. Julia felt a sickening lurch in her stomach and she froze for a moment, transfixed by their beauty, and the horror they represented. Tears trickled down her cheeks.

In a daze, she opened a bottle of Perrier water, poured a glass, and sat drinking it as the tears flowed. She glanced around half-heartedly, looking for Samantha's note, but it wasn't there. The maid must have thrown it out. Good. She didn't need to read it again. She remembered the words exactly and feared she'd never forget them.

The whole world, it seemed, had turned upside down and nothing made any sense. For the first time in her life, she'd fallen in love — not a little bit, but helplessly, passionately — with a woman, a woman adored by so many, she could have anyone she wanted. A woman who lived in America, for God's sake.

She had to clear her head. She went into the bathroom and had a shower.

And in one night, she thought, the woman she loved had broken her heart, and the painful ache in her chest was as powerful as the lustful ache in her thighs. That erotic ache, that in spite of it all, wouldn't go away.

The hot water surging over her felt soothing. It occurred to her that her entire being seemed to have become liquid — she didn't have substance anymore. She was wet with wanting, all the time, and now the tears that wouldn't stop.

She dried herself and began, with distracted, mechanical actions, to blow-dry her hair. Her brain seemed to have become liquid too. It didn't make any sense that when she was so much in love with Samantha, she'd slept with Lisa and physically wanted her. No, she thought, she hadn't wanted Lisa. Her body needed her, that was all. Her mind and body had diverged, and her body was obviously in charge. She couldn't trust herself to behave intelligently. She had to get out of there fast. She had to get away from Samantha.

She put on her makeup and dressed in her jeans and a dark green tank top. It was still dark, but it was going to be hot later, and even hotter where she was going. She put on her watch — it was four-thirty. She carefully packed up her notes and files and put them in her briefcase. She was methodical and took her time; there was no rush at this hour of the morning. She took her clothes out of the closet and drawers, placed them in her suitcases and cleared the bathroom of her cosmetics.

When everything was packed, she rang room service and ordered a light breakfast. After the coffee and toast, she felt better. The tears had stopped and she was purposeful. It was only five-thirty and too early to call the travel company she usually used, so she rang Qantas Airlines and booked a business-class seat on the next available flight to Bali.

At six-fifteen, the porter arrived to take her luggage downstairs and Julia cast one last glance around her room. She gazed at the flowers, felt her throat tighten and her eyes begin to fill again with tears. A sudden fury swelled in her chest and impulsively, she grabbed the flowers from the vase, took them outside to the balcony and threw them over the rail.

Shaking, she watched them land in the garden below and felt like a knife had been thrust into her heart.

By eight-thirty, Julia had checked in her luggage and passed through customs. Using her mobile phone, she rang Kerry at the hotel.

"Julia, where are you? I only just heard from Ruby that you checked out of the hotel this morning. She said she'd been trying to find you half the night!"

"Tell Ruby I'm sorry if she's been worried. I won't be back, Kerry. Something came up and I had to go. If Adele calls you, tell her I'll phone her later today. Don't forget the shots we still need. You know what to do."

"Yeah, of course, but —"

"You'll be back in the office on Monday and I won't be there to see the proofs, so I want you personally to select the best shots, okay? You know what I want. Don't let Adele choose them."

"What'll I tell everyone here?"

"Tell them goodbye for me and that I'm sorry I had to leave so suddenly."

"What about Samantha? What'll I tell her?"

Julia felt a painful grip in her leaden stomach and tears stung her eyes. She swallowed hard. "Tell her thanks for the flowers."

Julia said goodbye to Kerry, then rang Gum Nut cattery and extended Magpie's stay for a couple of weeks.

She turned off her phone, dropped it into her briefcase and boarded the plane.

Julia descended the aircraft steps and walked across the tarmac to the terminal building at Denpasar, the capital of the Indonesian island. The sweet, heavily perfumed, steamy air enveloped her, filling her with a sense of peace. It was one forty-five in the afternoon. Julia glanced at her watch, still set on Australian time. It was three forty-five there.

She hadn't made any arrangements for accommodation, but knew the heavy tourist season hadn't yet begun and was sure she'd get a room at her favorite hotel. She hired a taxi and began the hour-long trip up into the mountains, heading for the artists' village of Ubud.

She relaxed in her seat and watched the streets of the city quickly dissolve away into lush, green farmlands and rice-paddy fields. As they climbed higher up into the mountains, the hillsides became terraced with rice paddies and crops. She saw women walking along the roadside, balancing baskets of bananas, coconuts, avocados and bright red rambutans on their heads. Through tropical foliage she glimpsed decorative stone walls, draped in bougainvillea, surrounding home compounds. A young man, a sarong tied at his waist and red flowers in his hair, shepherded noisy geese along the road. Brilliantly colored ducks were swimming on rice paddies sparkling in the sun.

They arrived in Ubud and passed by the crowded market in the main street. Minutes later, the taxi turned into the gravel driveway of the hotel, which consisted of a group of small bungalows nestled into a hillside. Small paths led through the thick foliage of frangipani, hibiscus and bougainvillea to each of the private bungalows, and to the open-sided, thatched-roof dining pavilion.

There were plenty of vacancies, so Julia chose a bungalow close to the spring-fed swimming pool that was constructed on one of the garden terraces close to the river.

Hot and tired, she sat down on a cane chair on her veranda and gazed across the river at an ancient Hindu temple. She could hear the tinkling of bells, strains of haunting musical instruments, and glimpse the movement of people beyond its stone walls. They must be preparing for some kind of celebration tonight, she thought.

She placed her glass of iced water on the low table nearby, where, arranged on a small bed of leaves, was a religious offering of rice and flowers to appease hostile spirits, and beside it, incongruously, was a telephone.

With a melancholy sigh, Julia's thoughts returned to the realities and responsibilities of her life. She would have to phone Adele soon and explain what was going on.

She had been pushing all thoughts of Samantha to the back of her mind for hours, but suddenly her mind was filled with her. Beautiful memories of Samantha's face, Julia's kissing her, and Samantha's hands touching her, alternated with horrible images of the flowers and the note. Her body ached with desire while tears of pain and anguish ran down her face. Julia wondered how long she would feel this way, how long she could stand it.

Although the temperature was cooler in the mountains than in coastal Denpasar, the jungle-like landscape increased the humidity; the heat was more oppressive. She went inside to the dark, relative coolness of her bungalow, peeled off her damp, sticky clothes and put on her bikini.

She walked down the short flight of stone steps, brushing past a riot of hibiscus flowers, to the edge of the pool. There was no one else around as she dived into the fresh cool water.

* * * * *

"I'm outta control, Ruby. I've lost it. Look at me! I can't go on tonight, I just can't." Samantha's eyes were puffy and tearful.

"Come on, honey, you can get through tonight. We've got a rest day tomorrow and you can deal with all this then." There was a knock at Samantha's door and Ruby opened it to Danny.

"How's it all goin'," he said brightly. "The local reviews for last night's show are great, just great!" He slid one hand into his pocket and paced up and down, stroking his hair. "Just one more concert on Saturday night and then it's home sweet home."

Samantha turned her gaze wearily from the open balcony doors to Danny and took a sip of her drink. She wasn't in the mood for his exuberance. "For God's sake, slow down, honey."

He stopped dead in his tracks. "Shit! What the hell's wrong with you?" Samantha bit her lip and stared into her glass.

"She's all in knots about Julia."

"Oh, yeah, right. It's a real shame the way she took off like that." He resumed his pacing, shooting her an embarrassed glance. "I had no idea, you know . . . you and her." He cleared his throat. "I didn't know she meant that much to you — personally, you know."

Samantha said softly, "Well, she does."

"Yeah, well, I've got some great news that'll cheer you up. I've just fixed a great deal for an Atlanta concert in two week's time. The promoters are calling it 'Samantha Knight Comes Home.' It'll be a one-night-only show and tickets go on sale tomorrow."

Samantha gulped down the rest of her bourbon

and gazed through the doors. She didn't want to be reminded again that she was leaving in a few days' time, without even knowing where in the world Julia was.

"It'll be a total sell-out, of course. They're plannin' on a crowd of ten thousand!"

"That's real good, Danny. But why don't we talk about it later when Sam's a bit more interested, okay?" Ruby opened the door for him.

"Oh, yeah, right." Still looking bright-eyed, Danny paused in the doorway. "I'm arrangin' with Adele to use one of those shots Kerry showed me, as a publicity poster. She got some great shots — really great!"

"Great, honey. See you later." Ruby closed the door behind him and shook her head in exasperation. "God! Sometimes that man is hard to take."

Ruby sat on the sofa beside Samantha and put her arm around her. "I didn't expect her to take it so badly, Ruby. Do you think she hates me for sending that note?"

"Well, I think if she was gonna hate you, she wouldn't have taken off like that, she would've waited around last night for you to come back. If I was in her position, I would've hung around so I could throw the flowers in your face and tell you to shove the goddamn things up your ass! That's what I would've done, honey." Samantha smiled weakly through her tears. "I'm sure she doesn't hate you. More the opposite I would think. Now, get ready, girl. We're onstage in an hour and a half." Ruby headed for the door.

* * * * *

Like a black silk shroud, night was falling softly over the mountains, and the tropical creatures of the night were beginning their wistful calls. Julia was sitting on the veranda of her bungalow. Still in her bikini, she was sipping an ice-cold glass of wine.

There were lanterns bobbing about within the temple's walls, and the strains of the music were more clear. It was a mysterious and melancholy sound. With the fragrant breeze caressing her skin, she closed her eyes and, for a little while, was able to empty her mind of her troubles and listen to the rhythms from the temple and the night insects. Then, somewhere not too far away, monkeys began screaming in disagreement, bringing her thoughts back to earth.

It was eight-thirty on the east coast of Australia. She picked up the phone and rang Adele at home.

She could hear Adele take a deep drag of her cigarette. "So, tell me you're tracking down a story that's going to be the biggest scoop in the history of entertainment journalism." This was followed by a short, hacking cough and another deep inhale.

"I'm afraid not. I just had to get away in a hurry. It was personal."

"Where the hell are you, anyway?"

"Bali. But I don't want anyone to know that. I've arranged with Kerry to get the final shots we need and I'll finish the story over the next couple of days. I'll e-mail it to you, if I can get a line, or fax it or —"

"For Christ's sake, Julia! I'm not worried about any of that! What's going on with you? When can I expect you back? We've got some big stuff coming up — I need you here."

"I just don't know. I'm a bit confused at the moment. I don't even know if I want to come back to

141

the magazine just yet. I'm sorry . . . I just don't know."
Julia struggled to hold back the tears that threatened
to overwhelm her. She heard the click of Adele's gold
lighter and another deep inhalation.

"Did you have some sort of argument with
Samantha Knight? She rang me twice today asking
where you were."

Julia turned her face away from the receiver and
wiped at the tears pouring down her face. She
swallowed and tried to compose herself. Then,
impulsively, she decided to tell Adele the truth.
Everyone she knew was going to have to find out
sooner or later that she'd changed, that she was a
lesbian. That was an issue not confined to her
relationship with Samantha. Adele may as well hear it
from her first. She took a deep breath. "Samantha and
I began an affair. It didn't work out and I'm trying to
deal with it."

"Fuck!" A coughing fit was followed by silence for
a few moments, broken only by the sound of Adele's
furious smoking. "Look, I don't want to hear any
suggestion of your leaving the magazine. You take as
much time as you need to deal with . . . you know,
whatever you have to deal with. Maybe you just need
a change, a new challenge."

God! I think I'm already having that! There was
another long pause.

"I'm always buying story items from overseas and
paying too bloody much for them. Maybe you'd like to
work somewhere else for a while. That'd suit the
magazine fine if you wanted to do it."

"I don't know, Adele, but thanks. I'll think about
it." Julia promised to keep in touch, and they said
goodbye.

Julia went inside her bungalow and pulled on a T-shirt and jeans, then wandered along the winding stone path, lit by tiny lanterns, to the dining pavilion.

She didn't feel much like eating, and pushed her spiced rice and chicken around her plate. The laughter and conversation of the other guests faded into the background as she imagined Samantha onstage tonight. She could envision every expression of her beautiful face, hear every nuance in her sultry voice, and she longed to be with her. She wondered if Samantha was feeling miserable, missing her too, or whether she was just feeling guilty. Samantha would only be trying to find her, Julia thought bitterly, to convince her of her point of view. Samantha said in her note that she wanted them to remain friends, but that, Julia decided, was not an option.

CHAPTER THIRTEEN

Samantha was sitting in her room late on Saturday morning, staring without interest at the TV, when there was a knock at her door. It was Ruby and Lisa.

"Come and have some lunch with us, honey. You can't stay cooped up in here all day again."

Samantha shoved her hands into the pockets of her bathrobe and slumped down heavily on the sofa. "No, I just don't feel like it."

Ruby sat on a chair opposite and rested her feet on the coffee table. "If Julia calls, she'll leave a message."

Samantha shook her head. "I spoke to Adele yesterday morning. She told me Julia's out of the country and doesn't wanna be contacted. I virtually begged the woman to tell me where she is, but she refused. I know Julia won't call now, but I wanna be here, just in case." Samantha glanced at Lisa who was standing just inside the doorway, examining with great concentration the button on her shirt cuff.

"You need some fresh air, girl! You stayed in here all day yesterday, all by yourself, and last night too. We missed you yesterday. We had a great time on the Gold Coast. I wish you had come with us, honey." Ruby yawned and stretched, her bracelets jingling brightly. "We stayed down there half the night. We found a dyke bar that was quite interesting. We had a great time, didn't we, Lisa?"

"Yeah."

Lisa was now taking an extraordinary interest in her watch. She was playing with the settings and the tiny beeps were getting on Samantha's nerves.

"Come on, honey. Get dressed and come out with us."

Samantha was only half listening. It occurred to her that she hadn't seen Lisa since Wednesday night, just before the concert started. Everyone knew that Samantha was worried sick about Julia's disappearance, and Lisa was the only one who hadn't asked her about it.

Lisa suddenly looked up at her with a startled expression, like a rabbit caught in a spotlight.

"Did you happen to see Julia on Wednesday night, Lisa?"

Lisa slipped her hands into her pockets and glanced away. Samantha's heart began to beat a little quicker. Lisa looked back at her and squared her shoulders. "Yeah, I saw her."

"Where?"

"In the bar downstairs around ten-thirty," she said defiantly.

Samantha felt a knot tightening in her stomach. "You were the last one to see her, and you didn't say anything? How was she? What did she say?" Ruby got up from her chair, slowly, and came and stood beside Samantha.

Lisa's eyes flickered from one to the other. "She didn't say anything. She'd drunk too much — she was crying." Tears sprang to Samantha's eyes and she felt sick. "I took her to my room and looked after her."

Samantha's head swam and she thought she'd faint. She felt her scalp prickle. She kept her voice low. "You looked after her? How?"

Lisa seemed to hesitate, then she shrugged and smirked. "For God's sake, Samantha, she spent the night with me. When I woke up, she was gone. Do you really want all the details?"

A blinding white light flashed before Samantha's eyes and instantly she shook with rage. She clenched her fists and lunged at Lisa. Ruby caught her wrist and held her tightly. Lisa side-stepped, looking shocked. Samantha yelled, "You fucking bitch! How could you do that! I'll fucking kill you!"

"It wasn't me who had her in tears!" Lisa yelled back indignantly. "I don't know what you did to upset her so much, but she didn't fucking leave here because of me!"

Tears were pouring down Samantha's face and she

thought she'd explode. She was struggling to get free of Ruby's grip. "I'll fucking kill you!"

"Get outta here, Lisa!" Ruby said. Lisa glared at them for a few seconds, then left with a slam of the door.

Ruby released her and Samantha flew at the door, pounding her fist into it. "I'll fucking kill her!" She stormed over to the bar and poured herself a bourbon. Shaking, she gulped it down and poured herself another. She stomped back across the room and was only half aware of Ruby grabbing the glass from her hand as she passed her. "How could Lisa have done that?" She shook her head. "I don't understand how anyone could be so heartless."

"She took her opportunity. That's the way she is."

Ruby was dialing the phone. Samantha realized she didn't have a drink and poured another one. Her head was spinning as she sank onto the sofa. Her mind filled with images of Julia with Lisa and the tearing pain in her chest was unbearable. She took a big sip of her drink. So, all that night when they were frantically looking for Julia, she was with Lisa — screwing Lisa. She couldn't stand it, and she started to cry. Ruby hung up the phone and went to Samantha, putting her arm around her.

"Why would Julia do that, Ruby?"

Ruby's tone was gentle. "Because she was distraught, confused, heartbroken, angry, or all of the above." She sighed. "That poor girl would've been in a bad way, honey."

"God, what have I done?"

"Well, girl, I think you fucked up big time, to tell

you the truth. You've broken your own heart as well as hers."

"I didn't expect it to hurt this much. I didn't expect her to react like this. I thought I was being so rational."

"Yeah, it's a real pain in the ass when people don't stick to the goddamn scripts we write for them, ain't it, honey?" Ruby shook her head. "Off they go, doing things and saying things that we didn't plan at all!"

"I wish I hadn't done it." The tears flowed unchecked down her cheeks and she felt herself unraveling. She went to gulp down the rest of her bourbon, but Ruby took the glass from her. "I want that, Ruby."

"Well, you ain't having it." Ruby got up and tossed it down the sink. "I've ordered you some lunch — salad and fruit juice. You're gonna make yourself sick if you don't eat."

Samantha blew her nose. "What am I gonna do?"

Ruby sat down opposite her. "Sam, you think you can arrange everything in your life just as easy as you can arrange your goddamn songs. You're in love with her, and you can't just make that go away because it's inconvenient."

"I wish I knew where she was. I wanna tell her I love her." Frustrated, Samantha sighed and pushed her hair off her forehead. "I can't bear this."

"Well, honey, it's about your timing. I think you might've lost your chance."

There was a knock at the door and Ruby got up to let in room service. She set out their lunch on the balcony table. "Come and eat, Sam. We've got a show to do tonight and you've gotta get your act together."

With a wistful glance at the mini-bar, Samantha

sat down at the table and, under Ruby's stern gaze, forced herself to eat.

The applause was thunderous and the audience was on its feet, demanding another encore. Bouquets of flowers and other gifts from the fans were being tossed onto the stage. A spotlight once again hit center stage, and Samantha ran out as the band began the intro to the new single from their album.

She could feel she had the audience in the palm of her hand. It had been hard work tonight, and she was glad they apparently hadn't noticed her performance wasn't what it should be. She beamed her warmest smile at them while the applause continued.

She knew Julia wasn't going to call. She was going back to Savannah tomorrow and feeling hopeless, she craved the comforts of home and her friends.

"Thank you. We've had a great time tonight." She began to sing, confident that the audience would never know her heart was breaking.

On Sunday morning, Samantha and the others congregated in the hotel lobby as their limo pulled up outside the main entrance. Lisa, who'd kept well out of Samantha's way since their altercation, had seen to it that their luggage and equipment had all been taken to the airport ahead of them.

A big crowd of fans and members of the local press shoved toward Samantha as the band made its way to the limousine. She smiled and spoke to as many of the onlookers as she could and signed some autographs. She really wasn't in the mood for it after another sleepless night thinking about Julia.

An hour and a half later, Samantha settled into her seat and waited for the plane to take off. She was glad to be going home, but this was the final cut with Julia's world and, it seemed, with Julia.

Julia was sitting alone in the dining pavilion at her hotel. It was already hot and a warm breeze was wafting through the thatched-roof building. Blossoms from a nearby shrub blew in and they tumbled across the floor. A few of the bright pink, perfumed flowers landed on her table. She steeled herself and sipped her strong Balinese coffee, trying to relax the tension that was increasing in her shoulders.

She wanted to forget the time but couldn't stop herself from continually glancing at her watch, still set on Australian Eastern Time, two hours ahead. The exact time of Samantha's departure was etched in her mind, and every nerve was focused on the moment.

When her watch finally clicked over to eleven o'clock, Julia closed her eyes and fought back the tears. Shaking, and she took a deep breath. *So, that's it. It's over.* Maybe now she could try to pull herself together. Since arriving on Thursday afternoon, she'd done nothing but lie around the pool, or lie on her bed, crying and feeling sorry for herself. She had been hiding away like an injured animal, she thought, and it was time to stop.

Back at her bungalow she left on her jeans and

changed her bikini top for her aqua camisole. She stood in front of the bathroom mirror, brushed her hair and applied some mascara and lipstick. It was the first time she'd bothered with makeup since she got here. She put on her dark, wrap-around sunglasses, grabbed her wallet and headed off along the winding stone path to the main road leading to the street market.

The marketplace was crowded with people — mostly locals but quite a few tourists as well. She passed displays of paintings, tables groaning with colorful wood carvings, and shops filled with rolls of batik fabric. She should buy a couple of sarongs, she thought. It was too hot to wear pants. She paused and browsed through a rack outside a shop. A beautiful middle-aged woman who was managing the shop smiled at her. "You come inside," she demanded. Julia obeyed her and emerged a short time later with six sarongs. She smiled as she continued down the street. If she went through her wardrobe at home, she could probably dig out a hundred sarongs she'd bought over the years. A teenage boy came up to her proffering an intricately carved wooden flute. Julia smiled and shook her head. She had quite a few of those at home somewhere too. He touched her arm to make her stop, then played something simple and sweet. He gazed at her with liquid eyes and grinned. Julia laughed softly, handed over the money and took the flute.

She decided to leave the market and head farther up the mountain to a restaurant she knew for lunch. She took the road through the monkey forest where the cool canopy of the trees was a relief from the hot sun. Hearing rustling above her head, she looked up to see three small monkeys swinging from branch to branch. They shrieked at her, and another one on the ground ran up and took a swipe at her shopping bag.

She felt better already. People got over broken hearts, and she would get over Samantha. She should try to put the whole thing down to experience. She had discovered passion and real love and heartbreak in two weeks — making up for lost time, she thought. She didn't want to love Samantha if Samantha didn't love her. The delicious ache of desire wasn't half as sweet when it wasn't returned.

She suddenly pictured herself kissing Samantha and felt a melting tremor. It would take a while longer, Julia realized, before she stopped wanting her.

She emerged from the shade of the forest onto an open road. The restaurant was set on the top of a hill just ahead of her.

She sat at a table near the huge picture windows. She could see a deep ravine, covered with rainforest, with the river winding and rushing below. A breeze blew through the open windows and the rattan fans overhead turned silently. The scent of sweet, tropical flowers mixed with the appetizing aromas of Nasi Goreng rice and satays cooking on the open grill. Listening to bird song wafting in from outdoors, Julia ordered a guava juice and chicken satay.

It was hard to imagine herself at home again, living a life that in any way resembled the past. Samantha was out of her life, but she'd changed Julia forever. Samantha had uncovered in her a depth of passion and an ability to love that she hadn't known were buried within her, and now she looked at life through different eyes. She suddenly felt afraid. At first she hadn't given a thought to the future, but when she fell in love with Samantha, she assumed Samantha loved her too, and nothing else had mattered. Beginning a whole new life as a lesbian would be very daunting without the woman she loved by her side.

God, Julia thought, maybe she shouldn't have told Adele about her affair. Everyone at the magazine would act differently toward her, and how would the friends she'd known for years react? Julia gulped down her cold juice and ordered another one. Her real friends would get used to the idea, she supposed. Besides, she would make new friends in time — other lesbians, if she could only find out where they were. She wondered if she would ever be attracted to another woman, then remembered Lisa. *God, why did I do that?* Julia must have been attracted to her on some level, which proved it was possible. She sighed. But it was going to be impossible to seriously want another woman while she was still in love with Samantha.

The waiter brought her lunch and she tried to enjoy the food while she turned her attention back to the view. Perhaps she could work as a free-lance travel writer. Then she'd never have to spend much time at home. She could avoid everyone and all their questions and just travel around the world. Or maybe she could rent a house in these mountains and hide away in this tranquil place forever. If she sold everything she owned, she could afford to live in Bali for many years. The idea was comforting, and she gave herself up to it for a while, imagining what her Balinese house would look like. She would grow a lot of purple bougainvillea, she thought, and frangipani, avocados, mangoes and coconut palms.

She finished her lunch. It was the first whole meal she'd eaten in recent days and she felt calmer. She ordered a coffee and watched a middle-aged couple, tourists, come in and sit down. They piled their bags full of souvenirs on the floor beside their table and took off their cameras.

The woman looked over at Julia and smiled. "It's just great up here, isn't it?"

Julia felt a cold shiver run down her spine. The woman's accent was just like Samantha's. Julia nodded and smiled weakly.

"Do you speak English, honey?"

Julia swallowed. "Yes." Her voice cracked.

"We're from Atlanta, you know, in the States. Where are you from?"

"Melbourne."

"Where, honey?"

"Australia." The woman seemed very friendly, but Julia couldn't stand listening to her soft, lilting accent. It was making her feel disoriented and she had to get out of there. She quickly put some money on the table. "Nice meeting you. Enjoy your stay." Julia grabbed her bag and left.

On the way out the door, she overheard the man comment quietly, "I thought Australians were supposed to be friendly . . ."

Julia headed back down the mountain to her hotel. Christ, she thought, it didn't take much to shake her up. *When would this be over?*

That evening she phoned home to check her messages. There was one from Ben, asking her to contact him urgently, telling her she was making a big mistake, and a couple of messages from friends with dinner invitations. But there was nothing from Samantha.

Angry with herself, she put down the phone. Of course, Samantha would know she wasn't home, so of course she wouldn't call there. But Julia had hoped, stupidly, that she might have left some kind of message. She reminded herself that Samantha wasn't going to leave the kind of message Julia wanted to hear anyway. Listening to Samantha telling her how this was all for the best wouldn't help at all. She promised herself she wouldn't check again.

CHAPTER FOURTEEN

It was a long and exhausting flight home for Samantha and the others. They flew via Sydney to Los Angeles, then went their separate ways. The three younger members of the band lived in L.A., Danny flew home to New York City, and Ruby and Samantha connected with a flight to Atlanta, where Ruby lived. Samantha had to pick up another flight from there to Savannah.

It was late on Sunday night, and very warm and humid, when Samantha's plane finally landed at the Savannah airport.

"Hey, gorgeous, we're over here!" Samantha turned toward the familiar voice. Tom and Mike were waiting for her in the arrivals lounge. It was a huge relief to see them and she hugged them both gratefully.

"Thanks for coming. You shouldn't have, it's so late." Tears sprang to her eyes. She enjoyed traveling, but whenever she'd been away for any length of time, she always found herself getting emotional when her plane touched down on her home turf.

"Don't be silly, sweetie. We couldn't have you coming all this way, then going home to an empty house alone, now could we?" Tom said as he gave her a hug. She couldn't help a fleeting thought about how, if things could have been different, maybe she wouldn't be going home alone.

Mike went off to collect her luggage while Tom told her how tired she looked, and how she needed some home-cooked dinners after months of restaurants.

Mike piled the suitcases into the car. "You must have tons of news, Sam. We read about how well you were received in Australia. See any kangaroos or koalas?"

Samantha laughed and rubbed her eyes as they began to drive home. "You may be surprised to learn, hon, that they don't actually have kangaroos hopping around the streets over there. We did see some at the zoo in Melbourne, though." Two days before she met Julia.

"More important than that," said Tom, "what are the women like over there. Any flings to report down under?"

Samantha felt her throat tighten. "There was one."
"And?"

Samantha bit on her lip to control her tears. "I don't wanna talk about it right now. I'll tell you about her later." Then she took a deep breath and told them a few stories from the tour.

When they pulled into Samantha's driveway, the automatic lighting around the house and garden made her grand old house look very welcoming, and she could see that the garden had been well tended by her gardener during her absence.

Using his own key, Mike opened the front door and took the suitcases upstairs. "The girls were in today," Tom said, "getting a few things ready for you."

Samantha went from room to room, glad to be back among her own things again. There were fresh flowers in vases around the house and food in the fridge. There was also a bottle of Champagne with an attached note from Donna and Candice: "Welcome home, Sam. Don't open this until we see you tomorrow. Can't wait to catch up. Love and kisses." The back garden looked green and lush, and the swimming pool was sparkling.

Upstairs, Samantha found her bed made up with clean sheets and there were fluffy towels in the bathroom. She was so tired, and distraught about Julia, that the display of generosity and love from her friends was all too much and tears welled up in her eyes.

"Oh, sweetie, what's wrong?" Tom asked as he put an arm around her.

"I don't know. I think I'm suffering from sleep deprivation, and everything's so nice. I'll be fine after I've slept for a month."

Samantha thanked them again and said goodnight,

then poured herself a glass of bourbon and, to relieve her aching muscles, decided to take a hot bath.

In the warm water, she sipped her drink and thought about how good it was to be back in her lovely house. She'd missed it. She really ought to finish the renovations on the place, she thought. There was plenty to be done restoring the intricate plaster work on the ceilings, re-polishing the timber floors and repairing the decorative trims on the verandas.

Julia would know exactly what to do, she thought. She'd know what colors to paint the rooms and what furniture and antiques to buy. Samantha closed her eyes and imagined how wonderful it would be for them to live here together. She knew Julia would love the house. They'd have so much fun fixing it up. If only it were possible, they would have a wonderful life together.

She finished her drink and got out of the tub. She wondered again where Julia was and what she was doing. With a sinking heart, she imagined that Julia would soon meet another woman and begin to forget her.

She turned back the covers on her big, antique brass bed and lay down, naked, on the cool cotton sheet. A light rain had begun to fall and she listened to the soft patter on the leaves outside her windows. The sound was as quiet as a whisper, and the sweet, fresh scent of moist earth and honeysuckle wafted through the open windows.

She looked at her bedside clock. It was one-thirty. It'd be around three-thirty Monday afternoon in Melbourne. She decided to call Julia before she went to sleep. It was probably a waste of time, but just maybe she'd be home or maybe she'd check her messages.

With a pounding heart, she listened to the phone ringing at Julia's house. It felt strangely like having contact with her, just listening to her phone. The machine picked up, and once again her eyes filled with tears as she listened to Julia's warm voice on the recorded message.

Samantha spoke with difficulty, trying to control the emotion in her voice. "Julia, I hope you're okay. I know you'll be angry with me, but I really need you to call me — I'm so worried about you. I miss you. I don't know what to do, but . . . I want you to know I love you. Please call me, baby."

Samantha fell back onto her pillows and let the hot tears fall. She imagined holding Julia in her arms again and making love to her. She ached with desire. If she only knew where Julia was, she thought, she'd jump right on a plane and go and see her. Eventually, she fell into an exhausted sleep.

On Monday night, Samantha went to dinner at Tom's and Mike's place. Donna and Candice were there and it was wonderful to be with them all again. Samantha felt happier and calmer than she had in days.

The evening was warm and they sat outside under the pergola that was dripping with cascades of yellow, sweetly scented Carolina jasmine. Samantha had brought the Champagne Donna and Candice left in her fridge, and they drank it while Samantha caught up with all the news and local gossip. The garden was filled with palms, ferns and flowers, and a small fountain trickled down a mossy rock garden into a goldfish pond. Samantha always admired their garden. Mike was a landscape designer and he had designed Samantha's garden too.

"I thought you might've been feeling homesick, sweetie," said Tom as he brought dinner to the table. "So I cooked you a traditional healthy, homey dinner."

Samantha gazed at the plates piled high with crispy chicken-fried chicken, French fries and corn fritters and wondered about "healthy." She couldn't remember when she last sat down to a meal containing so much fat. But Tom was a good cook and it looked yummy.

She smiled at him warmly. "It's just perfect, Tom. Thank you."

They helped themselves to food as Mike poured the wine.

"Now, before you tell us absolutely everything about the tour," said Donna, "we wanna hear about this special woman the boys said you mentioned last night."

Samantha's mind instantly shimmered with images of Julia. Everything would be perfect, complete, if only Julia were sitting beside her.

Samantha explained how they first met, her attraction to Julia and how it had all tumbled ahead rapidly, out of control, into a passionate mutual attraction that left Samantha hopelessly in love with her.

"I truly, stupidly believed that it would be better for us to end the affair before either of us got really hurt," Samantha explained. "But I made a big mistake. It seems I've hurt her dreadfully — at least,

I'm sure she's furious with me, and I feel like I can barely live without her. I still don't know how a relationship could work while we live so far apart, but I just know I'd be happier if I knew she loved me and that she was mine."

"Well, it would be goddamn hard to maintain a relationship under those circumstances," said Mike.

"But you've got three months off soon, haven't you, Sam?" Donna asked. "You could've at least spent *that* time over there with her. Although we'd miss you sorely," she added with a grin.

Candice looked at her with soft dewy eyes. "She'll contact you, honey. She just hasn't got your message yet. You've gotta give her a chance to get her head together and get home."

Samantha sipped her wine and felt sadness creep over her like a shadow. She pictured her sun-filled garden where she had been sitting that afternoon, day-dreaming about Julia. The long, late-afternoon shadows stalked across her lawn, swallowing the golden light inch by inch, and suddenly she'd felt an overwhelming sense of loneliness. The inviting, tranquil shade of the palms grew gloomy and ominous, and the brilliant colors of the flowers became dull and lifeless, and despite the heat, she shivered. She had wondered whether life without Julia would always feel like this.

"I'm worried that getting her head together will mean getting over me. I love her, but I'm selfish enough to not want her to meet another woman. And believe me, that's not likely to take long."

"For Christ's sake, honey, you're the first woman in her life. And the way you explain things, it sure sounds like she was falling in love with you," Candice said. "She's not gonna look at another woman for quite a while, I would say."

Samantha felt her heart leap to her throat as she remembered with breathtaking clarity, the moment when she discovered Julia had spent that terrible night with Lisa. She felt herself shudder with seething jealousy and wondered whether the others had noticed. Hadn't Candice ever heard of rebound romances? She couldn't bring herself to tell them about that.

"Just be patient, Sam," said Donna gently.

Tom laughed. "Patient! Samantha?"

The others all laughed too, making Samantha smile. She was glad the conversation turned then to her tour of Australia, and she settled in, determined to enjoy the evening.

For the rest of the week, Samantha relaxed and enjoyed her time at home alone, despite her anxiety and longing for Julia. She rang Julia every day, but Julia didn't answer or return her calls. She rang Adele again, too, but got nothing from her. If Julia heard her phone messages, Samantha's declaration of love obviously hadn't helped. But maybe she hadn't heard the messages. Samantha tortured herself constantly. She was unused to being in this position, unable to take control of events, and it frustrated her terribly. Ironically, Julia was in control now, and it felt like Julia was holding Samantha's life and happiness in the palm of her hand.

Samantha replayed the events in her mind over and over, trying to imagine what Julia might be thinking. She couldn't decide whether Julia was reacting out of pride and anger, or because she was deeply hurt. Most of all, Samantha was angry with herself. She had figured, when she sent the note to Julia, that Julia wasn't in love with her. She had ended the affair quickly to protect herself. Now, she hoped desperately that Julia did in fact love her and would forgive her. No woman had ever gotten to her like this before; she was obsessed with Julia.

She swam in her pool and often, on hot, steamy afternoons, sat in the garden reading in the shade of the banana palms. She had missed the flowering of the magnolias and they were growing heavy with lush, green leaves, and the last of the jasmine's spring blossoms were browning in the hot sun.

On Tuesday of the following week, three days before the Atlanta concert, Samantha spent the day in the music room, working on a song that had been swirling around in her head for days.

This was her favorite room in the house. Once it would have been used as a ballroom. Its proportions were perfect. As with the rest of the house, the floor was a beautiful quality hardwood. The fifteen-foot ceiling was embellished with original, elaborate plaster moldings, and the eye was drawn to the dominating, dramatically ornate window at one end that overlooked the front garden. To one side, there was some digital recording equipment, a simple mixer and a couple of guitars and a keyboard. Two comfortable sofas and a low table stood at one end, and near the window end of the room was her cherished Steinway grand piano.

The day was very hot and still, and the afternoon

sun blazed through the half-closed shutters, throwing long, golden streaks across the floor while Samantha sat at the piano. When she finished writing the song, a simple ballad, she recorded a rough arrangement onto disk, then she e-mailed the sound file to Ruby. Ruby would have enough time to play around with it before their rehearsal with the band on Friday. Samantha planned to perform the song in Atlanta on Friday night.

CHAPTER FIFTEEN

Julia swam to the stone steps and climbed out of the pool. It had been another hot, steamy day and it was still around ninety degrees. Not bothering with a towel, she wandered along the path back to her bungalow in her bikini, the water glistening in cooling droplets on her skin.

It was around ten o'clock on Wednesday night, and she wasn't ready for sleep. She sat on the veranda and poured a glass of wine from the bottle in the ice bucket on the table. She noticed that despite her constant use of sunblock, her skin was deeply tanned. That was inevitable, she thought as she sipped her wine, after two weeks of doing nothing else but swimming, lying by the pool and wandering around the town market.

She was feeling much more relaxed than when she had arrived, in a state of shock, looking for a place to hide away. The heat, peace and quiet had calmed her. She was feeling stronger and was no longer prone to unexpected tears. It was time to move on, she thought.

She gazed at the moths gathering and flicking around the light on the wall. Her longing for Samantha nonetheless remained. She couldn't help calculating what time it was in Savannah, and wondering what Samantha was doing, how she was feeling and who she was with.

The nights were the hardest, when she lay in her bed under the mosquito net, with only the eerie tropical night sounds for comfort. It was then, with no other distractions, that her mind was filled with Samantha. Every night she fell asleep burning with desire for her, and every morning she awoke from dreams of her. She realized that despite everything, the pain of the note — the rejection — had faded, while her love had grown stronger.

Suddenly, Julia's pulse quickened as everything came into focus. All she really wanted in the world was to be with Samantha. The vague ideas she had about career or lifestyle changes were irrelevant. It was Samantha she wanted.

Agitated, she got up and walked back down the path to the pool. She gazed at the moonlight shimmering on the water and watched the tiny gecko lizards calling in their strange clicking voices as they chased each other around the rocks.

She was in love with Samantha. She refused to give up on her this easily. She had no doubt about Samantha's desire for her, and she needed to find out if Samantha was in love with her too.

Samantha *had* loved her, she knew it. Her instincts were usually right. Maybe it was just that regardless of all her other strengths, Samantha lacked enough courage to deal with the problems their relationship might bring.

But she had the courage.

She made up her mind. She would fly to Savannah and see Samantha. She wouldn't call — she couldn't deal with this in a phone conversation. She'd leave tomorrow. After two weeks of feeling confused and helpless, she was suddenly filled with energy and purpose. It was a big step to take, to just arrive and present herself to Samantha, but Julia had to know whether her future was going to include Samantha or not. She needed to bring this period of limbo to an end.

As she got ready for bed that evening, she imagined Samantha agonizing over her decision to end their affair. Geography, the Pacific ocean — what a ridiculous reason. Julia smiled as she recalled Adele's offer. She could write for *The Entertainer* from the States. The magazine was always buying stories from there. If distance was Samantha's only problem, Julia thought, there was no problem at all. If Samantha wanted her, she would move there in an instant. She would have to take Magpie, of course, but those things could be arranged.

She felt impatient and couldn't wait to get there. She imagined holding Samantha in her arms, kissing her, and telling her everything was okay. With that wonderful image in mind, it occurred to her that Samantha apparently had a negative streak which Julia would have to watch in the future. With a contented sigh, she fell asleep.

On Wednesday night, Samantha had Donna and Candice over for a barbecue. She had set up the table beside the pool. She opened a bottle of Chablis for her friends, then put the steaks on the grill while she sipped her bourbon.

"God, it's so hot," said Donna. "I'm getting in the pool for a while." The high-walled garden was protected and private, so she pulled off most of her clothes and slipped into the pool in her panties.

"Sam?" Candice called from the kitchen which opened onto the garden, "where's the salad dressing?"

Samantha smiled. Whenever she had her friends over for dinner, they always fussed around in the kitchen because they believed she was totally incompetent where food preparation was concerned. Samantha knew she was no cook, but she was good at barbecues, and any idiot knew how to make a salad, for Christ's sake. "On the fridge door, hon," she called back.

A moment later, Candice came out onto the stone-paved patio looking distressed, holding the brand-name bottle of dressing at arm's length as if it contained strychnine. "Sam! I don't mean this crap. I've shown you how to make real dressing!"

"Oh, yeah. I forgot how to do it. Sorry." Samantha tried to look suitably chastised. Donna was chuckling. "Those bottles of things you bought for me are in there somewhere."

"Have you got any garlic and lemons?"

Samantha turned the steaks. "Ah ... no garlic, but there's a lime on the tree. Will that do?" Samantha picked the lime and handed it to Candice, who looked reasonably satisfied. She disappeared back into the kitchen.

Samantha picked up her glass of bourbon and went over to the pool. She was wearing an old pair of cut-off jeans and a tank top, and she sat on the edge of the pool dangling her legs in the water.

Donna emerged from an underwater swim. "You haven't mentioned Julia. I guess that means she hasn't called you, huh?"

Samantha shook her head slowly. "Nope. And I can't stand it for much longer."

"She probably hasn't heard your messages — that's the only explanation."

"Or she hates me, or she's met someone else."

"Sam, honey, you've got to imagine what it must be like for her. She's just figured out she's a dyke, falls in love, and right away she gets dumped! She hasn't even got a network of gay friends to turn to. She must be feeling awful."

Samantha felt a sickening grip in her stomach. She'd been plagued with the thought of Julia's feeling lonely and abandoned, and it worried her terribly. She was certain that was how Julia had ended up in Lisa's arms that night — there had been no one else for her. The horrifying thought occurred to Samantha that if she was feeling anywhere near as bad as Samantha was feeling, there might be a long line of Lisas in Julia's life until she got herself established into a gay lifestyle.

Samantha gulped down her bourbon. She suddenly felt furious with herself. "Tell me, Donna, why the hell I didn't imagine this outcome when I wrote that fucking note?"

"Maybe you didn't wanna see. Maybe you were too busy finding a way to avoid a difficult commitment."

Puzzled, Samantha looked at her. "What do you mean?"

Donna swam to the edge of the pool and picked up her glass of wine. She took a sip. "Well, look at your track record. Mandy's the most recent example. You two seemed really good together, but after a year and a half, you still wouldn't commit to her."

Samantha shrugged. "I just couldn't see any point in us living together, that's all. It would've been stupid for her to come and live here, away from her friends and her job in Atlanta when I'm away so much anyway. And there was no way I was gonna move out of here and live in Atlanta."

Donna rolled her eyes. "Hello! That's what I mean!" She drained her glass and held it out for a refill.

Samantha got the bottle of wine and poured her another. "I suppose you think Elizabeth falls into the same category."

Donna shook her head in a dismissive fashion. "That was all just plain silly. She had no intention of leaving her husband, and I'm sure you didn't really want her to."

"Yeah," Samantha mumbled. That's true, she thought, as she topped off her bourbon, adding some ice from the ice bucket. She slumped down in a chair by the pool. She had gladly ended her brief affair with Elizabeth, and although she was hurt and sorry to lose Mandy, it felt nothing like the way she felt about losing Julia. "The thing is — I didn't realize this before, or maybe like you say, I didn't wanna see — but I know now that I need Julia and I want her to need me. I never felt this way about anyone else before. And I can't stop worrying about her. Not knowing where she is or what she's thinking is eating me up." Samantha felt her throat tighten and tears suddenly well in her eyes.

"So, what're you gonna do about it?"

"Sam!" Candice yelled from the patio. "The steaks are starting to burn!"

"Shit!" Samantha raced over to the barbecue and grabbed the steaks. They were okay, luckily. She took them to the table as Candice brought out the salad.

Donna pulled on her T-shirt and sat down. "So, Sam, what're you gonna do?"

Samantha poured herself a glass of ice water from the jug and took a sip while she thought. She had to do something. She couldn't go on like this. She looked at her watch. It was eight o'clock. It would be ten o'clock Thursday morning in Melbourne. "I'm gonna phone her editor later tonight and *make* her tell me where Julia is. I'm gonna tell her it's a case of life or death, because it just about is." Samantha took a deep breath. "And then I'm gonna phone Julia again."

Candice and Donna thought this was a great idea if Samantha could manage to get the information, and while the conversation turned to other things, Samantha felt better at the thought of hearing Julia's voice, hopefully later that night. She didn't allow herself for the moment to dwell on the possibility that she might very well get a cold reception.

At seven o'clock on Thursday morning, Julia phoned her travel agent in Melbourne. It was nine o'clock there, and within a couple of hours, they called back with her flight details. She had to fly to Sydney to connect with her international flight, and as most of the flights out of Bali were fully booked, the earliest flight she could get left at eleven-thirty that night. She would stay overnight in Sydney, then fly to Los Angeles on Friday afternoon.

She was impatient for her journey to begin and couldn't bear the thought of hanging around the hotel for the rest of the day. She decided to leave straight away and spend the day in Denpasar. She made a quick call to Gum Nut cattery, extending Magpie's stay for at least another week, then quickly packed her things, settled her account and, at ten-thirty, loaded her luggage into a taxi and began the drive down to the coast.

At eleven-thirty, after Donna and Candice had gone home, Samantha sat down beside the phone with a glass of bourbon and phoned Adele Winters.

"How are you, Samantha? It's nice to hear from you. You'll be pleased to know the feature story is fabulous. I think it's one of Julia's best stories."

Samantha had almost forgotten about the story, and the thought that Julia had been somewhere in the world, writing about Samantha in recent days, made her tingle. "That's great, Adele." Her heart was pounding. She paused and swallowed. She could hear Adele light a cigarette. "Have you heard from Julia?"

"No, not a thing. But I told her to take her time."

Samantha noticed she had wound the phone cord tightly around her fingers and they were going white. "Aren't you worried about her?"

"No, she'll be fine."

Samantha felt a sudden anger. Adele had no goddamn idea what Julia was going through. *How the fuck could she say that?* "Well, I'm very worried and I wanna talk to her." Samantha knew her tone was terse. She could hear Adele drawing on her cigarette, and there was a moment of uncomfortable silence before Adele responded.

"My first loyalty is to Julia. She asked for her privacy." Adele sounded pretty terse too.

Samantha took a deep breath. She had to try not to scream at Adele, but if the woman didn't tell her where Julia was, she'd fly over there and fucking strangle her. The tips of her fingers felt cold and she unwound the cord to free them. "Please, Adele, you've gotta tell me how to contact her." She felt tears come to her eyes. "It's personal and important." There was another agonizing silence.

"Julia told me something about the personal situation that developed between you two."

"She did?" Samantha felt some relief. She hadn't wanted to give too much away and out Julia to her boss. The thought flashed through Samantha's mind that Julia's feelings for her must be quite serious if

she mentioned them to Adele. "Then you understand."
She heard Adele sigh.

"Hold on. I'll see if I can get her on the other line. I'll tell her you want to talk to her." Samantha heard a click and listened impatiently to the on-hold music, as she drained her glass of bourbon.

Why couldn't Adele just give her Julia's goddamn address? Julia might refuse to talk with Samantha and the call would have achieved nothing. She heard another click.

"She was in Bali, and believe it or not, she left only an hour ago. That would've been around ten-thirty there. The hotel says she took a taxi to the airport."

Samantha's heart began beating wildly. *Christ! Why didn't I ring earlier!* "When do you think she'll be home?" She asked breathlessly.

"They didn't know what flight she was on, but there are heaps of flights out of there, so she should be back sometime today. The flight takes about six hours."

"Thanks, Adele." After she hung up, Samantha gave herself up to the tears that she'd been fighting. Julia had been in goddamn Bali for the last two weeks. She must have felt so alone, Samantha thought. Maybe Julia hadn't checked her messages while she was away, and she'd call Samantha as soon as she got home.

She got herself another drink. She really ought to try and get some sleep, she told herself. Julia wouldn't be home for at least six more hours. But the knowledge that these long days of waiting to speak to her were within hours of being over made her too jumpy for sleep. She took her drink into the music room and played around on the piano, trying to distract herself.

Midnight — two p.m. in Melbourne. Julia wouldn't be home until around seven at the earliest.

Samantha went into the kitchen to make herself some coffee and took it out onto the covered patio. It was still very warm and raining softly. She gazed at the leaves of the banana palms glistening in the garden lights. They were bowed with the weight of the rain and it was dripping slowly off the ends of the leaves, as if they were weeping.

She finished her coffee and went inside. She poured herself another bourbon and wandered restlessly around the house. She imagined Julia arriving home and tried to remember details of Julia's house. She wished she'd seen the upstairs, so she would have more to remember. It would probably be cold; Julia would turn the heat on, and her little cat would run around excitedly, glad that Julia was home. She would've probably stopped on the way home and bought some food so she could cook dinner. Julia knew how to make salad dressing.

She went upstairs into a large airy room at the front of the house. Like much of the house, Samantha never used it. There was only an old Thirties sofa and two matching armchairs that once belonged to her parents. It had the solid but elegant rounded shape of the era and only needed recovering. The room offered a view of the peaceful, tree-lined street, and through the leafy gardens, it was possible to glimpse the lovely houses opposite. This would make a perfect study for Julia, Samantha thought. Her big oak desk would look great near the large shuttered windows Julia would like so much.

Samantha looked at her bedroom. This could be *their* bedroom. Julia might like to put her own beautiful chaise lounge between the two long windows. Samantha was suddenly swamped by erotic memories as she imagined them in this bed making love. She gulped the rest of her drink, trying to quell the tremors. She was making things harder for herself, having these fantasies. *I'm being stupid. I've been stupid all along!*

She went back downstairs to the kitchen. She had known from the moment she first saw Julia that she was special. She knew within a day she could fall in love with her, and she knew instinctively that the potential was there for Julia to want her. She probably fell in love with Julia at first sight, like Ruby said. Samantha had stood by, fascinated, in a kind of narcissistic daze while she witnessed and was drawn in by Julia's growing desire for her. She could have seized the chance of happiness for them both and concentrated on trying to plan a future with Julia, instead of focusing on the pain and disappointment that the future might hold.

Her head was beginning to ache. She needed to get some sleep, she thought. She went to the bathroom and took a shower, then got into bed. She glanced at the bedside clock before she turned off the lamp. One a.m. — at least four hours more to wait. She fell into a light, restless sleep.

Samantha gazed at the illuminated numbers on the clock. She was only half awake and for a moment felt disoriented. Then the numbers registered in her brain.

Four a.m. — six p.m. in Melbourne. Her head was splitting. She closed her eyes.

She was walking along a busy street when she saw Julia some distance ahead of her. She called out to her, but Julia didn't respond. Samantha began to run after her, but no matter how fast she ran, she didn't get any closer. Suddenly, the crowded street turned into a long, white stretch of beach and there was no one else around. She kept running after Julia and calling out to her. She noticed that Julia left no footprints in the sand. Then Julia stopped, and Samantha, breathless, ran up to her. Julia's eyes were focused on something behind Samantha, and it seemed Julia couldn't see her. Samantha began screaming desperately at Julia, but Julia couldn't hear her. Samantha reached out to touch her, and Julia disappeared.

Samantha woke with a start. She was sweating and her heart was pounding. It was five a.m. Julia should be home anytime now.

She went downstairs and filled the kettle to make coffee. The morning light was still thin, but it was warm and steamy from the rain during the night. While she waited for the water to boil, Samantha decided to take a quick swim. She grabbed a towel from the back of a deck chair on the patio, and naked, dove into the pool. The cool water cleared her head of the remnants of her troubled dreams and she tried to feel positive. She gazed at the streaks of pale pink and gold in the eastern sky and listened to the birds singing. The treetops were already bathed in sunshine, and she knew it was going to be another hot day.

* * * * *

Julia spent the afternoon looking around Denpasar, trying to control her impatience to begin her journey. Late in the afternoon, she stopped at a café, and grateful for the air-conditioned relief from the hot, grimy streets, she sat drinking an iced coffee. She calculated that it would be around five o'clock on Thursday morning in Savannah. Samantha would be fast asleep. She hoped Samantha was well and everything was okay for her, but she hoped desperately that Samantha was missing her too. She was happy to be taking some action at last, but shadows of doubt hovered. Samantha might not be as pleased to see her as she hoped. She had to fight against these doubts or she would lose her nerve. This was a chance, she told herself, that she had to take. The day after tomorrow, she'd know her future.

Wrapping herself in the towel, Samantha went inside and made the coffee. She took it outside and sat on a deck chair with the phone beside her. The clock on the kitchen wall read six-thirty — eight-thirty in Melbourne. Samantha dialed Julia's number. The machine cut in and Samantha left another message. Then she went upstairs, took a shower and got dressed.

Eight o'clock — ten p.m. in Melbourne. Samantha rang Julia's house again and when the machine cut in again, she slammed the receiver down. "You must be home!" she screamed furiously. "Stop punishing me — it's enough!" The tension released, Samantha broke down and cried bitterly. Julia would certainly be home and obviously didn't want to talk to her. She wasn't going to call. If Samantha had thought it was painful not knowing how Julia felt about her, knowing now that Julia didn't want her was agony.

The next day was Friday, and late in the morning, Samantha arrived in Atlanta. Danny and the other band members were due to arrive early in the afternoon. They were meeting at the concert venue for a lighting and sound check, plus a rehearsal. Ruby was waiting for her in the arrival lounge and they hugged affectionately.

"Let's go have an early lunch," said Ruby, as they headed off to collect Samantha's luggage.

Ruby's eyes widened as Samantha dragged two large suitcases off the conveyer belt. "I thought you were only staying at my place one night, honey. I didn't think you were moving in, for Christ's sake!"

Samantha laughed. "Don't panic. I'm only staying with you tonight. Then I'm flying out first thing tomorrow morning to Australia." Ruby looked stunned. "Come on, I'll tell you about it over lunch. I wanna know what you've been doing for the past ten days."

They sat in their favorite diner and ordered burgers.

"So, what're you up to, girl?" Ruby looked like she was about to burst with curiosity. She swept her hair back in a quick agitated gesture, accompanied by what sounded like an unusually cacophonous jangle.

She filled Ruby in on her call to Adele on Wednesday night, then said, "I spent most of yesterday feeling desperate. I've never felt so depressed in my life. But by last night, I made up my mind that I couldn't leave things this way." Samantha played with the straw in her glass, bending and creasing it. "I knew I'd spend the rest of my life phoning Julia and having a relationship with her goddamn answering machine." She paused to drink some Coke, first removing the split and useless straw from the glass. "I've been going crazy, Ruby. It got so I built my days around my calls to Julia! So, I decided I just had to go there and see her."

Ruby shook her head as if she didn't hear correctly. "You just told me that Julia's been home for at least a day and a half, has obviously heard the messages you left for her every day for ten days, and she hasn't called you. So you wanna fly all the way there and see her? That's a hell of a long way to go, honey, to have a door slammed in your face!"

Samantha fiddled with her hair and tried to maintain her confidence. "She won't do that. Not when she sees me."

"I know you're good-looking and charming, but you might need a little more than that," said Ruby with a grin.

Samantha felt a lump in her throat and her eyes filled with tears. She bit on her lip to control herself.

Ruby suddenly looked anxious and stroked Samantha's arm. "I'm sorry, honey. I was only fooling around."

Samantha swallowed hard. "I know, but you're right. I keep having terrible moments of doubt. Who do I think I am, for Christ's sake? What makes me think she loves me after what I did, or even actually loved me before? Julia could have anyone." She looked up at Ruby through her tears. "I keep imagining her falling into my arms, but why would she?"

Ruby's voice was gentle. "Because you're wonderful and generous and sincere and she'd be crazy not to fall into your arms. But I just want you to be ready in case she *is* crazy and says no."

"I'm hanging on to the belief that in this short time, her feelings for me couldn't have gone. I wanna believe she's just being very proud or very stubborn, and if only I can tell her I'm sorry, I'm sure it'll all be okay." She paused and took a deep breath. "If I'm wrong, she'll have to tell me to my face. That would be extremely hard to take, but at least then I could learn to let her go."

"Is it a good idea to travel there on your own? What about the press giving you a hard time?"

Samantha sighed impatiently. The last thing she wanted to worry about were practical considerations. Being rational had got her into this mess in the first place. "Without any publicity hype, no one will notice me traveling on my own. I'll be okay."

"Well, honey, I think it would be better to wait this thing out, but I know you, and you've gotta do it or you'll never rest easy."

Samantha nodded and felt another twinge of anxiety.

"I like that song, by the way," Ruby said with a smile. "I've worked out some nice harmony to run behind the verses, to make it all sound distant and kind of dreamy."

"Sounds great." Samantha felt more tears spring to her eyes.

"So, honey, tell me what you and your little clique of Savannah queers have been up to."

Samantha was glad to change the subject and felt her nerves settle as they talked about other things for a while before they left to meet the others for the rehearsal.

Julia landed in Los Angeles, mid-morning on Friday. She was tired from the long flight, but the anticipation of seeing Samantha kept her adrenaline flowing.

She had a two-hour wait before the connecting flight to Atlanta. She used the airport facilities to have a shower and change into clean clothes she had in her hand luggage. She put on her black linen fitted pants and a white, sleeveless, silk top, dried her hair, put on her makeup, and decided she felt almost human again.

She spent the rest of the time drinking coffee and trying to read yet another paperback she picked up in the airport gift shop. Doubts came into her mind occasionally and gripped her with a sickening dread. She kept reminding herself to be positive and to trust her instincts.

By the time her flight landed in Atlanta that evening, Julia felt decidedly nervous. This was Samantha's part of the world, and the moment of truth wasn't far away. There was just one more leg of the long journey left; the flight to Savannah leaving later that night.

She grabbed a handful of pamphlets from the tourist desk and leafed through them, looking for hotels. She'd be able to find a room for the night in one of them, she thought, and then tomorrow, when she was feeling refreshed after a decent night's sleep, and hopefully had her wits about her, she would take a taxi to Samantha's house.

She sat in the cafeteria drinking more coffee and was suddenly seized with panic. Maybe coming all this way had been a waste of time, she thought. Maybe she should have phoned instead. She knew the band was due for a long break after the Australian tour, but what, for God's sake, made her think Samantha would be home? She could be anywhere.

Julia felt breathless, the knot tightening in her stomach. Even worse than Samantha's not being home, she thought, was her being home but not alone. Maybe she'd met someone else. Julia ran her hands through her hair and took a deep breath. She was over-tired, she told herself. Of course Samantha wouldn't have met someone else in two weeks. She had to believe Samantha loved her or she wouldn't be here.

She looked around for a distraction. "For God's sake, get a grip," she muttered to herself. She saw a newspaper stand and, grabbing a paper, slowly turned the pages, trying to take an interest in Atlanta's local news.

She turned another page and almost fainted in shock. She gazed in disbelief at a full-page photograph of Samantha. It was the beautiful shot that Kerry had taken at the Opera House, during those moments when her life had changed forever. It was an advertisement for a one-night concert tonight in Atlanta. Her hands shook. She checked her watch. The show would be more than half over.

"She's great, isn't she?" Julia jumped. A woman

clearing a table beside her was looking at the page. "I wanted to go to that concert, but it was sold out."

"Was it?" Julia mumbled distractedly. Her mind was spinning, but she was tired and felt muddled. She had to get to the concert. She grabbed her bag and raced around to the airline desk.

"I have to cancel my flight," she blurted, placing her ticket on the desk. The attendant looked at it and began punching information into his computer. Julia was shaking and her heart was pounding. She wondered how long it would take a taxi to get there.

"Well, ma'am, your luggage is already on board the aircraft and we can't unload —"

"Forget it." Julia ran outside and grabbed the first taxi off the rank.

CHAPTER SIXTEEN

As the taxi drove away from the stadium, Julia
stood for a few moments outside the entrance,
listening to the muffled screams and applause.
Samantha was in there, she thought, so close, but the
huge building and what sounded like an enormous
crowd were an impressive, inhibiting barrier. She
glanced at a group of women standing nearby.

"We got here too late," one woman said to her.
"They had some last-minute tickets, but they're all
gone. Ten thousand, they sold."

God, Julia thought, getting in there was the next problem. She picked up her bag, took a deep breath and walked inside.

Immediately, she could hear the rhythms of the music she knew so well. She walked past the closed box office and headed toward two suited ushers who were standing by one of the doors leading into the auditorium.

She gave them a confident smile and produced her Australian press card. "You've got no idea how hard it's been to get here. I thought I'd never make it at all." One young man looked at her credentials.

"Have you got a ticket ma'am?"

Julia thought rapidly. She was in a hurry to get in there, and probably the quickest way to get this over with was to appeal to his masculine ego. She gave her hair a toss and adopted what she hoped was a sweet, winning smile. She fluttered her eyelashes a little because she knew it worked. "Look, this is terribly embarrassing, but I seem to have misplaced the ticket. In the rush to leave Australia and get here on time, I think I must've left it behind." The two men hesitated. She smiled and fluttered some more. "I've just traveled across the world to get here."

In the background, the music stopped and thunderous applause erupted. "There's not a lot of point in bothering now, ma'am. You're only gonna catch the encore."

Julia's heart was pounding. "That's okay." She picked up her bag. They stepped aside and opened the door for her.

Julia entered the darkness of the auditorium and stood spellbound as she gazed at the stage. The band was there waiting in the half-light — Samantha was offstage, and the audience was standing, cheering and applauding, demanding her return.

Julia descended the steps leading to the press seats. Not surprisingly, there were no seats left, so she stood against the wall at the end of a row which ran along one side of the stage. The subtle, midnight-blue backdrop slowly changed to deep purple streaked with hot pink downlights. Four spotlights suddenly beamed onto the center of the stage, converging into one pool of light. Smoke wafted in the powerful lights, creating a surreal effect, then from stage left, Samantha walked out into the spotlight. There was an upsurge in the applause.

Julia's eyes filled with tears as she gazed at Samantha. She looked so beautiful, she was breathtaking. She was wearing the same outfit as the night when Julia first saw her.

The crowd quieted and sat down. Samantha laughed her seductive, throaty laugh, and Julia felt herself go into meltdown. "Thank you. You've been a wonderful audience. It's great to be home, and we've had a really great time playing for you tonight." The audience cheered and applauded. Samantha waited until they quieted down completely, then with her mouth close to the microphone, she said in a low, sexy voice, "God, it's so hot in here, don't you think?" Slowly, she slipped off the black jacket, tossing it to one side, and stood there in tight, shiny black pants and a skimpy, shimmering pink bikini top. Ten thousand fans went wild.

Enraptured, Julia watched her. It seemed incredible that she and Samantha had been lovers. Remembering the way this gorgeous woman had touched her, what her exquisite mouth and hands had done to her, seemed like an unbelievable, erotic dream.

"Here's a song from our last album!" The band crashed in with a popular rock song that had the women in the front rows up and dancing in their seats. Samantha moved around the stage with agility and grace, the perspiration glistening on her skin, and Julia craved the sweet, salty taste of her. She looked so radiant and happy, it was hard to imagine that she had missed Julia at all.

The song ended and eventually the applause subsided.

"Just before we go, I've got a special song I'd like to sing for you that we haven't performed before. It means a lot to me and I hope you like it."

As the background lighting slowly changed to emerald and dark blue, Ruby began playing the introduction on the keyboards. A lighting effect created a sea of twinkling lights, like thousands of tiny stars constantly moving over the whole stage. The crowd was hushed, the atmosphere electric with anticipation. Julia's heart was bursting with love for Samantha, but she'd never felt so removed from her. Samantha seemed remote and untouchable.

Jenny came in on rhythm guitar and Louis on bass. Samantha spoke again — her voice low and husky, "This is 'Julia's Song.' "

Julia's head swam — she thought she'd faint. In her pure, powerful, velvety voice, Samantha began to sing:

"I thought fire and water could never mix
But since I met you babe I know that ain't true.
I drowned in the ocean of your eyes

While I was on fire for you.

"I thought the ocean was too wide
And the waves of passion too great.
The emerald ocean of your eyes
I was too weak to navigate.

"I abandoned you my love,
I jumped ship to save my skin
But now, I'm washed up on the rocks
And I've lost everything within."

Ruby, Jenny and Louis added vocal harmonies and
Don added percussion in the chorus. Tears were
pouring uncontrollably down Julia's face.

"Now the sadness floods my soul
But babe, I've paid for my sin.
I've cried an ocean of tears
And now I've learned how to swim."

Throughout the song, a spotlight swept slowly
across the audience. As she sang, Samantha followed it
around the auditorium, directing her performance to
individual women as the light paused on them for a
few moments.

"The truth cut me like a knife,
Your honesty was so raw.
But you're in my blood now, honey
And I want you even more.

"I abandoned you my love,
I jumped ship to save my skin

But now, I'm washed up on the rocks
And I've lost everything within.

"Forgive me, baby, for leaving you,
This fire's raging out of control.
Take me back, honey, you've got my heart
And I offer you my soul.

"I need you, darling,
I'll swim with the tide
The only truth is in the pools of your eyes.
Only your love can touch me now
Everything else is lies."

Julia could hardly believe the words she was hearing. They expressed Samantha's love for her more forcefully than Julia could ever have dreamed.

The spotlight slowly swept around to the side of the stage, creeping along the row of press seats until the light settled on Julia.

"I abandoned —"
Samantha gasped. She froze, and for a moment she completely forgot where she was. She couldn't believe her eyes. Julia was like a vision out of a dream. Her heart was nearly beating out of her chest and she stood, mesmerized, while the band played on without her.

The spotlight suddenly left Julia, and Samantha, totally disoriented, turned to Ruby. Ruby was singing the chorus with the others and she smiled and nodded, indicating she'd seen Julia too. A repeat of the chorus was coming up, and still looking at Ruby, Samantha shook her head helplessly. She couldn't stop the tears, and she felt like she was about to break down.

Ruby took up the lead vocal and Samantha turned back to the audience. She put her hand over her eyes and tried desperately to compose herself while Ruby sang.

"I'm sorry," Samantha said over the band.

The audience began applauding her and cheering. They seemed to be moved by her emotional display.

The sound mixer pulled back the level of the band, while Samantha spoke again. "I'm really sorry. I can't go on." The audience applauded and screamed louder. Women at the front showered the stage with flowers. "Thank you. Goodnight."

The band kept playing and the audience kept screaming as Samantha clipped her microphone onto its stand and walked off the stage.

Julia hurried past the seats in her row, filled with people staring at her, and raced up the steps and out the main door. She stood looking around, wondering how to get backstage, when a woman with long, brown hair ran up to her. She was wearing jeans and a T-shirt with SAMANTHA KNIGHT COMES HOME emblazoned across it.

"You must be Julia," she said with a grin. "I'm Paula. Sam sent me to get you." Julia followed her to a door which she opened with a key, down some stairs and along a few narrow corridors. Above them, the band was playing one of their old hits with Ruby singing. They came to another door. "She's in there. See ya later." Paula continued on down the corridor.

Trembling, Julia stared at the door. She could hardly believe Samantha was just on the other side. She opened the door and Samantha turned to her. Julia thought her knees would give way.

Samantha swept her into her arms, pulling her inside and closing the door. Tears trickled down Julia's face and she couldn't speak. Samantha gazed at her for moment, looking stunned. Then she gently pressed Julia up against the back of the door and kissed her with a passion that set Julia on fire. Julia's hands glided over Samantha's back and shoulders and she felt Samantha's heart pounding against her body.

Samantha looked at Julia with tears in her eyes. "I can't believe you're here. I've been so miserable without you, it was killing me." She kissed Julia again. "I'm so sorry, baby, I made the biggest mistake of my life. Promise me you'll never leave again."

Julia was dissolving in Samantha's arms, and she murmured against Samantha's mouth, "Promise me you'll never send me irises again."

Samantha smiled weakly through her tears. "I don't care what it takes or what I have to do." They kissed. "We have to be together." They kissed again. "We'll find a way, won't we?"

"Yes, darling, don't worry, I already have." Julia was in a daze. All she wanted to do was make love to Samantha. She was vaguely aware that the music overhead had stopped and that the audience was applauding.

"Come on, baby, let's go." Samantha slipped on her jacket and grabbed a bag from the floor. "Paula's waiting for us in a car out back." She took Julia's hand and opened the door. Julia looked at her, bewildered. "We've got a plane to catch, darlin'. I've got a big old house to show you, with shutters on the windows." Samantha smiled one of her sexy half-smiles. "I'm taking you to Savannah."

CHAPTER SEVENTEEN

It was close to one o'clock in the morning when the taxi pulled into the driveway of Samantha's house. Julia's luggage had been held at Savannah Airport, and while the driver took their suitcases up to the veranda, Samantha watched Julia walk toward the house, slowly, hesitantly, then stand in silhouette against the lights gazing up at it. It was a clear, moonlit night, still and steamy. Samantha paid the driver and the taxi drove away.

During the half-hour flight from Atlanta, they'd held hands while Samantha listened, enraptured, to

Julia's story about Bali and her travels across the world to be with her. With her deep tan accentuating the stunning color of her eyes, her chestnut hair shining and glinting with a few sun-lightened streaks, Julia was more beautiful than ever. And each time Julia paused, gazing seductively into her eyes, Samantha became momentarily breathless with desire. When Julia told her about the magazine offer, and she realized Julia could stay, that they could live together permanently, she was overcome with tears. She could hardly believe it was all happening, and she had never felt so happy in all her life.

Julia hadn't said anything and Samantha suddenly felt anxious. She tried to see the house through Julia's eyes. What if she didn't like it? She didn't want her to be disappointed. She wanted everything to be perfect for her. She went to Julia and took her hand. "Let's go inside, baby."

Julia smiled. "The house is beautiful, darling."

"It's okay if you don't like it. We can get another house — any house you want." Julia kissed her cheek as Samantha unlocked the door.

"God," Julia breathed as she walked into the vast entrance hall. She seemed transfixed by the grand staircase. "It's more beautiful than I imagined."

Samantha sighed in relief. Julia was looking even sexier than she remembered, and she ached to sweep her into her arms and take her straight to bed. But she should let Julia take a look around, she told herself, let her get used to it all. She went to her, slid her arms around her waist from behind, burying her face in Julia's hair. "Do you want a drink or something, honey?" She felt Julia shudder. She turned in Samantha's arms and gazed into her eyes.

She gave her hair a little toss. "I want something," she whispered. Her expression was determined, lustful, and Samantha trembled. Julia unzipped the black, shiny jacket, pushed it off Samantha's shoulders to reveal the pink bikini top, then trailed her fingers across her nipples.

Samantha shook as a fire suddenly swept through her. She kissed Julia passionately. "Maybe you'd like to see upstairs first," she murmured.

The room was dappled in moonlight; it streaked across the bed. Julia's tanned body was shadowy against the white sheet, the light skin in the shape of a tiny bikini, offering erotic guidance for Samantha's mouth. Her arms were outstretched, her eyes unfocused with desire, she was breathing quickly. Her legs were apart, one knee drawn up, and her body was saying, take me.

In a rush of passion, Samantha kissed her, savoring her luscious mouth. Julia returned the kiss hungrily, arching her body against Samantha's. She moved her mouth to Julia's breasts, breathing in her heavenly perfume, and took one rosy nipple into her mouth, sucking it gently. Julia gasped. Unable to wait any longer, Samantha moved between Julia's legs, placed her hands beneath her hips, raising her to her mouth. She slid her tongue between her thighs, and Julia groaned. She was soaked. Samantha's mouth and cheeks were wet with her as she stroked and pushed her tongue inside her. She moaned, realizing how much she'd been craving the taste of her.

Julia's body tensed, and Samantha quivered with her own tiny contractions as a surge of lust pumped through her. Then Julia's hands were in her hair, pressing Samantha's mouth hard against her as she arched her hips. "God," she cried out, and her body shook with powerful tremors.

Samantha took her in her arms. Julia was trembling, her heart pounding, and Samantha kissed her. She thought she would completely melt away with love as she licked away Julia's tears.

Julia sighed and stroked Samantha's back and hips, sending electric charges coursing through Samantha's body. She kissed Julia's throat and shoulders softly. "You should go to sleep now, baby," she whispered. "You must be exhausted."

Julia smiled and shook her head. She trailed her fingers across Samantha's back, and around to her stomach, then reached down into the silky wetness between Samantha's thighs. Samantha gasped, and Julia trembled with a renewed rush of desire as she felt a fluttering contraction against her fingers. "Lie down for me, darling," she said quietly. "Let me do everything I've been dreaming about for the last two weeks."

With a groan, Samantha rolled onto her back. She gazed into Julia's eyes and gave one of her sexy smiles. "Why do I always find you so persuasive?"

Julia smiled again, then ran the tip of her tongue across Samantha's nipples. Samantha quivered, whimpering. Julia gave her hair a little toss, and adopting her best Southern belle accent, she said, "Well, honey, I really wouldn't know."

OVER THE LINE by Tracey Richardson. 176 pp. 2nd Stevie
Houston mystery.   ISBN 1-56280-202-X $11.95

JULIA'S SONG by Ann O'Leary. 208 pp. Strangely
disturbing . . . strangely exciting.   ISBN 1-56280-197-X   11.95

LOVE IN THE BALANCE by Marianne K. Martin. 256 pp.
Weighing the costs of love . . .   ISBN 1-56280-199-6   11.95

PIECE OF MY HEART by Julia Watts. 208 pp. All the
stuff that dreams are made of —   ISBN 1-56280-206-2   11.95

MAKING UP FOR LOST TIME by Karin Kallmaker. 240 pp.
Nobody does it better . . .   ISBN 1-56280-196-1   11.95

GOLD FEVER by Lyn Denison. 224 pp. By author of *Dream*
Lover.   ISBN 1-56280-201-1   11.95

WHEN THE DEAD SPEAK by Therese Szymanski. 224 pp. 2nd
Brett Higgins mystery.   ISBN 1-56280-198-8   11.95

FOURTH DOWN by Kate Calloway. 240 pp. 4th Cassidy James
mystery.   ISBN 1-56280-205-4   11.95

A MOMENT'S INDISCRETION by Peggy J. Herring. 176 pp.
There's a fine line between love and lust . . .   ISBN 1-56280-194-5   11.95

CITY LIGHTS/COUNTRY CANDLES by Penny Hayes. 208 pp.
About the women she has known . . .   ISBN 1-56280-195-3   11.95

POSSESSIONS by Kaye Davis. 240 pp. 2nd Maris Middleton
mystery.   ISBN 1-56280-192-9   11.95

A QUESTION OF LOVE by Saxon Bennett. 208 pp. Every
woman is granted one great love.   ISBN 1-56280-205-4   11.95

RHYTHM TIDE by Frankie J. Jones. 160 pp.   . . . to desire
passionately and be passionately desired.   ISBN 1-56280-189-9   11.95

PENN VALLEY PHOENIX by Janet McClellan. 208 pp. 2nd
Tru North Mystery.   ISBN 1-56280-200-3   11.95

BY RESERVATION ONLY by Jackie Calhoun. 240 pp. A
chance for true happiness.   ISBN 1-56280-191-0   11.95

OLD BLACK MAGIC by Jaye Maiman. 272 pp. 9th Robin
Miller mystery.   ISBN 1-56280-175-9   11.95

LEGACY OF LOVE by Marianne K. Martin. 240 pp. Women
will do anything for her . . .   ISBN 1-56280-184-8   11.95

LETTING GO by Ann O Leary. 160 pp. Laura, at 39, in love
with 23-year-old Kate.   ISBN 1-56280-183-X   11.95

LADY BE GOOD edited by Barbara Grier and Christine Cassidy.
288 pp. Erotic stories by Naiad Press authors.   ISBN 1-56280-180-5   14.95

CHAIN LETTER by Claire McNab. 288 pp. 9th Carol Ashton
mystery.   ISBN 1-56280-181-3   11.95

NIGHT VISION by Laura Adams. 256 pp. Erotic fantasy romance
by "famous" author.   ISBN 1-56280-182-1   11.95

SEA TO SHINING SEA by Lisa Shapiro. 256 pp. Unable to resist
the raging passion . . .   ISBN 1-56280-177-5   11.95

THIRD DEGREE by Kate Calloway. 224 pp. 3rd Cassidy James
mystery.   ISBN 1-56280-185-6   11.95

WHEN THE DANCING STOPS by Therese Szymanski. 272 pp.
1st Brett Higgins mystery.   ISBN 1-56280-186-4   11.95

PHASES OF THE MOON by Julia Watts. 192 pp. . . . . hungry
for everything life has to offer.   ISBN 1-56280-176-7   11.95

BABY IT'S COLD by Jaye Maiman. 256 pp. 5th Robin Miller
mystery.   ISBN 1-56280-156-2   10.95

CLASS REUNION by Linda Hill. 176 pp. The girl from her past . . .
                                                    ISBN 1-56280-178-3   11.95

DREAM LOVER by Lyn Denison. 224 pp. A soft, sensuous,
romantic fantasy.   ISBN 1-56280-173-1   11.95

FORTY LOVE by Diana Simmonds. 288 pp. Joyous, heart-
warming romance.   ISBN 1-56280-171-6   11.95

IN THE MOOD by Robbi Sommers. 160 pp. The queen of
erotic tension!   ISBN 1-56280-172-4   11.95

SWIMMING CAT COVE by Lauren Douglas. 192 pp. 2nd
Allison O Neil Mystery.   ISBN 1-56280-168-6   11.95

THE LOVING LESBIAN by Claire McNab and Sharon Gedan.
240 pp. Explore the experiences that make lesbian love unique.
                                                    ISBN 1-56280-169-4   14.95

COURTED by Celia Cohen. 160 pp. Sparkling romantic
encounter.   ISBN 1-56280-166-X   11.95

SEASONS OF THE HEART by Jackie Calhoun. 240 pp. Romance
through the years.   ISBN 1-56280-167-8   11.95

K. C. BOMBER by Janet McClellan. 208 pp. 1st Tru North
mystery.   ISBN 1-56280-157-0   11.95

LAST RITES by Tracey Richardson. 192 pp. 1st Stevie Houston
mystery.   ISBN 1-56280-164-3   11.95

EMBRACE IN MOTION by Karin Kallmaker. 256 pp. A whirlwind
love affair.   ISBN 1-56280-165-1   11.95

HOT CHECK by Peggy J. Herring. 192 pp. Will workaholic Alice
fall for guitarist Ricky?   ISBN 1-56280-163-5   11.95

OLD TIES by Saxon Bennett. 176 pp. Can Cleo surrender to a
passionate new love?   ISBN 1-56280-159-7   11.95

LOVE ON THE LINE by Laura DeHart Young. 176 pp. Will Stef
win Kay's heart?   ISBN 1-56280-162-7   11.95

DEVIL'S LEG CROSSING by Kaye Davis. 192 pp. 1st Maris
Middleton mystery.   ISBN 1-56280-158-9   11.95

COSTA BRAVA by Marta Balletbo Coll. 144 pp. Read the book,
see the movie!   ISBN 1-56280-153-8   11.95

MEETING MAGDALENE & OTHER STORIES by
Marilyn Freeman. 144 pp. Read the book, see the movie!
                                        ISBN 1-56280-170-8   11.95

SECOND FIDDLE by Kate Calloway. 208 pp. P.I. Cassidy James
second case.   ISBN 1-56280-169-6   11.95

LAUREL by Isabel Miller. 128 pp. By the author of the beloved
Patience and Sarah.   ISBN 1-56280-146-5   10.95

LOVE OR MONEY by Jackie Calhoun. 240 pp. The romance of
real life.   ISBN 1-56280-147-3   10.95

SMOKE AND MIRRORS by Pat Welch. 224 pp. 5th Helen Black
Mystery.   ISBN 1-56280-143-0   10.95

DANCING IN THE DARK edited by Barbara Grier & Christine
Cassidy. 272 pp. Erotic love stories by Naiad Press authors.
                                        ISBN 1-56280-144-9   14.95

TIME AND TIME AGAIN by Catherine Ennis. 176 pp. Passionate
love affair.   ISBN 1-56280-145-7   10.95

PAXTON COURT by Diane Salvatore. 256 pp. Erotic and wickedly
funny contemporary tale about the business of learning to live
together.   ISBN 1-56280-114-7   10.95

INNER CIRCLE by Claire McNab. 208 pp. 8th Carol Ashton
Mystery.   ISBN 1-56280-135-X   11.95

LESBIAN SEX: AN ORAL HISTORY by Susan Johnson.
240 pp. Need we say more?   ISBN 1-56280-142-2   14.95

WILD THINGS by Karin Kallmaker. 240 pp. By the undisputed
mistress of lesbian romance.   ISBN 1-56280-139-2   11.95

THE GIRL NEXT DOOR by Mindy Kaplan. 208 pp. Just what
you d expect.   ISBN 1-56280-140-6   11.95

NOW AND THEN by Penny Hayes. 240 pp. Romance on the
westward journey.   ISBN 1-56280-121-X   11.95

HEART ON FIRE by Diana Simmonds. 176 pp. The romantic and
erotic rival of *Curious Wine.*   ISBN 1-56280-152-X   11.95

DEATH AT LAVENDER BAY by Lauren Wright Douglas. 208 pp.
1st Allison O Neil Mystery.   ISBN 1-56280-085-X   11.95

YES I SAID YES I WILL by Judith McDaniel. 272 pp. Hot
romance by famous author.   ISBN 1-56280-138-4   11.95

FORBIDDEN FIRES by Margaret C. Anderson. Edited by Mathilda
Hills. 176 pp. Famous author's "unpublished" Lesbian romance.
                                               ISBN 1-56280-123-6   21.95

SIDE TRACKS by Teresa Stores. 160 pp. Gender-bending
Lesbians on the road.   ISBN 1-56280-122-8   10.95

HOODED MURDER by Annette Van Dyke. 176 pp. 1st Jessie
Batelle Mystery.   ISBN 1-56280-134-1   10.95

WILDWOOD FLOWERS by Julia Watts. 208 pp. Hilarious and
heart-warming tale of true love.   ISBN 1-56280-127-9   10.95

NEVER SAY NEVER by Linda Hill. 224 pp. Rule #1: Never get
involved with . . .   ISBN 1-56280-126-0   11.95

THE SEARCH by Melanie McAllester. 240 pp. Exciting top cop
Tenny Mendoza case.   ISBN 1-56280-150-3   10.95

THE WISH LIST by Saxon Bennett. 192 pp. Romance through
the years.   ISBN 1-56280-125-2   10.95

FIRST IMPRESSIONS by Kate Calloway. 208 pp. P.I. Cassidy
James first case.   ISBN 1-56280-133-3   10.95

OUT OF THE NIGHT by Kris Bruyer. 192 pp. Spine-tingling
thriller.   ISBN 1-56280-120-1   10.95

NORTHERN BLUE by Tracey Richardson. 224 pp. Police recruits
Miki & Miranda — passion in the line of fire. ISBN 1-56280-118-X   10.95

LOVE'S HARVEST by Peggy J. Herring. 176 pp. by the author of
Once More With Feeling.   ISBN 1-56280-117-1   10.95

THE COLOR OF WINTER by Lisa Shapiro. 208 pp. Romantic
love beyond your wildest dreams.   ISBN 1-56280-116-3   10.95

These are just a few of the many Naiad Press titles — we are the oldest and
largest lesbian/feminist publishing company in the world. We also offer an
enormous selection of lesbian video products. Please request a complete
catalog. We offer personal service; we encourage and welcome direct mail
orders from individuals who have limited access to bookstores carrying our
publications.